I0581486

Dark Tidings

Jess Charle

Cover Art: Meghan Mazzarisi

Cover Design: Joshua Feliz

Reviewers: Julia O'Connell and Jonathan Harbaugh

Author Photo: Alexander Wozniak

Special thanks to Josiah Robinson, for listening to my dark tales and helping me unveil the perfect adjectives to best horrify.

ISBN-13: 978-1-7376819-3-9

Printed in USA

Dark Tidings

Jess Charle

Contents

The Twelve Days of Christmas

TW: See Trigger Warning Appendix

"Even though I was with Marcus, I wanted Nate to notice me. I didn't realize that it's not always nice to feel wanted. I have my boyfriend — sorry — ex-boyfriend, to thank for teaching me that."

I wanted to stop the tape, remind her to stay focused, but I could already tell this statement was going to be a long one. This was far from how I wanted to spend Christmas day but I understood that she needed to tell someone the whole story, her story, and it wasn't worth it to rush her.

"Marcus isn't bad… I wouldn't have dated him if he was bad," she emphasized the word as if it were a sliding scale and 'bad' was the extreme, "but, I guess I'm not as good a judge of character as I thought." She looked pained.

I cleared my throat. She sighed and looked back up at me, "I started dating Marcus about a year ago," she thought for a moment, "Yeah, pretty much exactly a year ago. He had been crushing on me for… well for forever. My long-term boyfriend had broken up with me the week before our office's annual Christmas party—I remember because I was annoyed I didn't have a date to go with. So…" her face scrunched as if she tasted bile at the back of her throat and was about to be nauseous, "I drunkenly made out with Marcus under the mistletoe. It was late and I was a mess. But the next morning I woke up and Marcus had bought coffee and a croissant from the bakery down the block. We didn't even have sex, he had just… put me to bed. He even slept on the couch. Yeah, he's a little… 'obsessive,' but…" you could hear the air quotes, "he's sweet. Or, at least I thought he was. He took care of me and… and I guess that was the first time a guy's ever really done that. And, well," she paused, "I guess that's what I needed. I am almost forty and, as my mother constantly reminds me, I'm not getting any younger."

I nodded, feeling more like a therapist than a police chief. I touched the button on the side of my phone, seeing if there was any word. Wondering if I would be more needed else-where. But it was Christmas and the force was out seeking a homicidal maniac, for the first time with an actual lead, so I sat back and continued to listen to Ms. Monroe's story.

Her eyes were locked on the back of a picture frame on my desk. It was a picture of Myra, my wife. Bridget's eyes were focused but also, not… They were focused on the black back of the picture, but her mind was far, far away. I resisted the urge to take the photograph, to hide it in my desk drawer, to keep her cold, focused eyes away from my wife. I thought of Myra, pictured her sitting on the couch watching *Love, Actually* for the third time this season. God, I hate that fucking movie.

"Then I met Nate." her voice was breathy and her eyes grew dewy at the mention of his name. She was still staring at the back of my wife. The back of her picture. Before I could stop it, my hand shot out and nudged the picture forward, towards me. Bridget looked up at me, startled, the spell broken.

She blushed slightly and continued, "Nate started working at our company a few months ago as the IT guy. His official title was help desk specialist or something." She waved away the nonsensical phrase as if it irritated her, "He replaced Terry, who left to go work at some stupid startup that I know will be bankrupt in six months if it isn't already."

She had said Terry's name as if it had coated her tongue in an unpleasant lemon flavor. Apparently, Ms. Monroe did not approve of Terry. Her nose was turned up into a sneer as if he were the human equivalent of discovering shit on the sole of your shoe. She leaned in towards me, her eyes looking up at me conspiratorially as she lowered her voice, "He was a Republican." she quickly sat back upright and looked at me gravely. I nodded my head as if in understanding. There was no need to tell her that I too, was a Republican, and no, I am not a piece of shit, but thanks.

She nodded back at me, her focus loosening again as if her hate of Terry had been the only thing normalizing the situation. She stared down at her fingernails. "Nate is..." she trailed off, picking under her thumbnail, "he's perfect."

She looked up at me, not sheepishly like I would've expected, but with a sad kind of longing that made her look much younger than she was.

"He's young and handsome. Smart, kind. He's the drummer in some rock band. I've dragged Marcus to a few of their shows." She gave her fingers a small secret smile. "They're terrible." her voice was light with laughter. The voice that people use when discussing the quirks of someone they love. "He just... he has so much life. So much character. I can feel him enter the room without seeing him, without hearing him. I can sense his presence."

She looked up at me and we stared at each other for a moment. I had nothing to add to this schoolgirl crush, so I did what years in the force could never teach me but two daughters and wife could: I stayed quiet and waited.

"See, Marcus doesn't really have any hobbies. He doesn't even have a favorite type of movie. It's not that we disagree on whether to watch a romantic comedy or an action film, he just has no opinion. He watches what I want to watch and likes what I like. Unless you consider painting tiny figurines of wizards and dragons as a passion," she snorted.

I did consider that a hobby, but I didn't say anything.

Her blue eyes danced above my head as she eyed the dusty corners of the small beige office. I sat patiently, waiting for her to continue. She didn't. There was a reason why deputy Black wanted me to conduct this interview.

I cleared my throat, "and Nate is the man you believe to be in mortal danger, correct?"

She nodded, her eyes widening with fear, "Have they found him yet? Have they found Marcus? Is Nate ok?" Raw anxiety made her voice jagged and harsh.

I touched my phone again, out of habit more than anything. I knew I hadn't received any updates.

"No news yet, but we've got almost the entire force out tonight. We're doing everything we can to prevent another death. In the meantime, please continue with your stor—" I cleared my throat again, stopping the word short, "statement."

"I should have broken up with Marcus. It would've been the adult thing to do. Break up with Marcus, ask Nate out, then go from there. But I'm an idiot, a coward... an idiotic coward." She looked exhausted, "I didn't want to break up with Marcus, because…" her eyes darted to the side of the desk, "I wasn't sure Nate was into me and I didn't want to be alone."

I nodded.

"But that's why I think he's in trouble." her voice was louder, stronger. Her tone serious, grown confident with fear.

"I know, Ms. Monroe. We're doing everything we can. Please, tell me about the gifts you mentioned earlier."

"Yeah, the gifts." she shuddered slightly, almost imperceptibly, "I think Marcus knew I was into Nate. I mean… I tried to hide my crush. Like I said, I don't even know if Nate thinks of me that way, so I try to treat him like just another co-worker. I guess more than just a co-worker, but still just a friend." she looked briefly guilty, then continued, "I started getting small presents last Thursday, December 14th." She nodded towards the charm bracelet sitting in an evidence bag on my desk, "The day of the first murder."

I couldn't stop the image from flashing into my mind: Helen Roger hanging limply from one of the tall oaks in the park. A jogger had found her body at about 8 am during his routine morning run. Her neck had broken with the impact. A coldness crept towards my spine as I thought of her pale face. Her eyes were much too large, bulging from their sockets. They were turning a white I never want to see again. Her pupils grey, gone forever into the void.

I ignored the cold sweat forming on my brow and took a large silent breath to slow my heart rate before I asked, "What was the present exactly?"

Bridget tapped the evidence bag with a long fingernail painted a festive red, "It was the bracelet and the partridge in a pear tree charm."

Helen's swollen filmy eyes floated back into my mind. I steadied myself and swallowed, "And you think the charm was a message? That Mrs. Roger was the partridge in a pear tree?"

Bridget nodded, "I didn't realize at the time, but now it makes sense. It's a pattern."

"You mentioned a note before, but you no longer have it, is that correct?"

"Yes. The box was sitting on my desk when I showed up for work, wrapped in soft pink paper. There was a note that read

'To my true love on the first day of Christmas.' And it was signed, 'your admirer.'"

"But you didn't keep it?"

"I... I didn't want Marcus to find it."

"Why not?"

"I didn't want him to get jealous."

I studied her for a moment, one eyebrow raised, "And what made you believe that Marcus wasn't your 'admirer?' Wouldn't that have been your first suspicion?" Now I was the one with air quotes in my voice.

She shrugged, "I didn't think Marcus was creative enough to do something like that. He bought me socks for my birthday. A bracelet, let alone a charm bracelet, wasn't like him." She picked at her nail, eyes trained on a coffee stain in front of her, "But I guess I was wrong."

"What did you do with the bracelet?" my internal voice chided me for asking the question since it was more out of personal curiosity than professional necessity.

"I hid it in my desk drawer."

"So Marcus wouldn't find it?"

She nodded.

"And you continued to receive these… presents. One every day, correct?"

"I didn't realize they were connected to the murders until yesterday."

"I understand, Ms. Monroe. You had no reason to suspect anything. Please describe each gift for me. In the order you received them. They're all here in the evidence bag, correct?" I asked.

"Yes, they're all there." I noticed her gaze traveled everywhere but the bracelet, sitting between us like a disowned child. "I received the charm with two turtle doves that Friday."

"December 15th," I added.

She nodded, "Like the first gift, it was sitting on my desk when I arrived in the morning, wrapped in pink paper. It was the same day you found that couple."

Mrs. and Mr. King had been found that morning at the bird sanctuary up the river. The caretaker had discovered them. They were both in their late twenties, married for four years. Mrs. King's mother explained to me on the phone later that day that they were truly in love with each other, her voice wet with tears. I didn't tell her that they had been found naked, Mr. King positioned on top of Mrs. King in a staged act of intercourse. The wooden handle of a small knife sticking out from her breast.

"Cause of death for Mr. King was poison, surprisingly enough." The coroner told me. Surprising because poison victims weren't often staged like that. Staged as a calling card to the cops, or a threat to the victim's family, or an insult to the victims themselves. Or maybe just as a giant 'fuck you' to the living.

"Was Mrs. King poisoned as well?" I asked.

The coroner shook her head, "No, she died from the stab wound. I'd say about a half-hour after her husband died." She picked up the picture of the bodies from the crime scene, examining it like one would a painting at the Louvre, "It's a macabre Romeo and Juliet. Him poisoned, her stabbed. Taking her life to follow him into death."

"Why position them as if they were having sex then?"

She looked up at me, her forehead scrunched in thought. Finally, she said, "I think it's one final expression of their love for each other."

I shook my head in disagreement, "No, that's not it… love can't be staged by a madman. I think… I think it's a power thing. Like rape. He forced them to make the ultimate sacrifice as lovers and then forced them into a position of intimacy and love. A scene that should be personal and private, but he put it on display."

"Their love raped and soiled for the masses," she nodded.

"And then the next day you received the charm of the french hens," I said, no longer asking. The story obvious from there.

Bridget nodded, her face pale.

The sisters. Three elderly sisters had been abducted from Sandy Hills Retirement Home early December 16th. Sometime after 3 am according to the nurses on the night shift, one of which had helped the eldest sister use the restroom around 2:45 am. Their bodies were quickly discovered in the manger scene outside of St. Peter's downtown. They had been positioned so that they were kneeling around the statue of baby Jesus.

Their faces were bruised, their ankles tied tightly together behind them and their wrists tied in front. The soft skin of their inner forearms turned up towards the sky, long red lines forming angry crosses on each of their wrists.

They had been murdered there, in the manager, their blood painting the holy scene. Large sticky pools had formed around the crib. The smell of hot iron filled my nostrils like angry bees attacking my sinuses. It was then that talk of a serial killer began to echo through our minds, our meetings, and the media around us, leaking out to the city and creating fear and panic during the happiest time of the year. The theatrics alone connected the murders, despite each victim and scene contrasting drastically from each other. Until this month, three murders in as many days had been unheard of in this small city.

"Then on December 17th, you received the four calling birds charm?"

The children's choir. He hadn't killed just four, he had killed all seven. None of them had yet seen their thirteenth year. Their choir director found them in the school's auditorium where they were going to rehearse for the Christmas show. Their tongues had been cut out, fishing line threaded through the tips to form a loop so the sick bastard could hang them from the tree that decorated the left side of the stage. Their bodies sat on the benches where they would've sung that very night, blood staining the metal ridges on each surface, so thin and close together that the blood would be impossible to completely remove. The overflow dripping from the open sides of the benches fell to the polished wooden floor with a thick drip. Drip. Drip.

"There was a note with that one," tears formed around the edges of Ms. Monroe's eyes. She cleared her throat and recited, "four calling birds, voices sweet as honey, pure as snow, for my true love, may I admire the echoes of your song for years to come."

"And let me guess, you threw that note out too?"

"I didn't realize…"

"It's ok, Ms. Monroe. I believe you."

On December 18th, Mr. Harold Goldberg was found slain in the backroom of his jewelry store, his throat cut from ear to ear. All his fingers had been removed except for his thumbs and each digit was placed in one of the candlestick holders of the menorah on his desk. Blood coagulated at the base of the gold symbol for divine wisdom. The coroner informed me that his fingers had been removed before his throat was cut.

"I didn't realize…" she repeated.

On December 19th we received a call from a house off of Longfellow road. The owners of the home were in the process of finishing their basement and the construction workers had arrived that morning to find human intestines hung along the bare rafters like Christmas garland, small twinkling lights wrapped around them, winking at their audience. When we arrived the men showed us to a section of brick wall that had not been completed the night before, the mortar still fresh. It took three hours for us to catalog and then remove the bricks, careful not to disturb the body we knew would be inside. One of the men identified him for us: their contractor, Peter Zinferd. There was a large cut from his sternum to his genitals, the skin of his stomach open like the cardboards walls of an advent calendar, exposing his empty insides.

"I didn't realize…"

Elizabeth Turner, lead ballerina for the community theater's upcoming production of Swan Lake, was found December 20th floating in a fountain in the middle of the park. She bobbed in the red water like a lifeless buoy. Her feet had been cut off pre-mortem.

Bridget began to sob.

Two women were found brutally dismembered in a room at the Bentliff Inn downtown on the 21st. They were only identifiable by their shredded maid uniforms clinging to what remained of their torsos. Jill Thompson and Mary Higgins had come in to work at 8 am that morning and were found at 10 am. It turned my stomach to think of how the bastard could have done it so quickly without anyone seeing.

Ms. Monroe's body heaved up and down, her slim shoulders shaking with the force of her cries which echoed off the plaster walls of the small office.

We still hadn't been able to identify the girl we found in the alley on the ninth day. She was outside the emergency exit of

Tiger's Paw, a dance club near the heart of the city. Her head had been removed, her neck now a jagged raw mess. She was wearing a tight black dress and strappy heels. I imagined that all she had wanted was a night of thoughtless fun, a night to lose herself to overpriced alcohol and loud music. Maybe even lose herself to the sexual embrace of another. Yet, instead, she has lost all identity. Without a face, it was difficult to estimate her age, but I could tell she was young. Probably about the age of my eldest who just celebrated her twenty-first birthday in November.

Bridget sniffed loudly, "I should've noticed. I should have realized Saturday. That… that poor man." Tears streamed down her face. She couldn't continue. Mr. Jason Larson, the manager at the big box store. His eyes had been gouged out and shoved deep down his throat, his heart removed. Using a sharp blade, the killer had cut a deep slit into the base of the organ, which was placed with care at the top of a Christmas tree in the display window.

"I should've realized the connection!" Bridget cried suddenly, startling me. "I should've seen it!" her voice rose with a cry.

She stopped and inhaled sharply, trying to stop herself from hyperventilating but it was too late. I stood and was beside her in two steps. I placed my hand on her back and lowered my face so it was level with hers, "Ms. Monroe, it's ok. Try to hold your breath. That will slow your body and hopefully your breathing."

Bridget closed her mouth, her lips pressed tightly together. Her body shook with the effort but she locked eyes with me and refused to let herself breathe.

"Good. Very good, Bridget." I patted her on the back softly. After a few moments, she let the air inside her lungs escape with a violent explosion. But she was able to inhale deeply and slow her breathing. "Better?" I asked.

She nodded and I returned to my seat. She looked shaken. Both her hands cradled the styrofoam cup of coffee in front of her, her knuckles turning white with her efforts to stop them from shaking.

"Hindsight is 20/20." It was a stupid thing to say, but it's all I had.

Mrs. Monroe straightened, "I… I didn't realize it until the next day." Her throat was tight and the bottom of her right nostril glistened with snot. She inhaled deeply as she tried to resolve herself, then continued, her voice still weak, but calmer. "There was a note on the eleventh day. It came with the charm: a small silver woman holding up one of those flute things you always see Peter Pan or Peter Piper with - I can't remember which. Then I saw all these Facebook posts about her, the girl, Piper." Tears started to blur her words again, her voice rising an octave, "She was only six years old." A sob choked in the back of her throat before she collapsed onto the desk, her arms around her head as if she were a child.

Piper. Poor Piper. So little and frail. Her mother reported her missing at 4 pm after trying to pick her up from school. She had waited in the pick-up lane for ten minutes before asking one of the teachers supervising if her daughter was running late. The teacher went into the building and returned moments later to say that Piper's teacher had seen her leave the classroom at her usual time. The mother, Mrs. Carol Dosher, immediately panicked. Staff searched the school for the young girl but she was nowhere to be found.

We came as soon as we were called, hyped up on the knowledge that someone was going to die that day.

Her body wasn't discovered until 5 am Christmas morning. This morning, even though it already felt like days ago. A fisherman saw her as he was walking down the pier. He had pulled her out of the water, a job I'm ashamed to admit I'm glad I avoided. She had been tied to the leg of one of the docks, so the fisherman had to cut the ropes with his jackknife. He apologized to me through tears, explaining that he was so panicked he hadn't noticed as his knife cut dull grey lines into her thin arms. Dark blood oozed out lazily, stiff from the cold and the absence of a heartbeat.

The coroner said that she had been alive when the murderer left her.

"Would she have frozen to death before the water got to her?" I asked, trying to keep the hope from my voice. Trying to sound professional. My thoughts screamed at the heavens, begging them that the child went from the numb death of freezing. That she hadn't been conscious all night screaming herself hoarse as the water slowly rose around her. As unfamiliar fingers of frost reached up her neck, searching patiently for a way to invade her small body, to take it as their own.

The coroner avoided my gaze as she left the question unanswered. I tried to remember how old her son was. Probably not much older than Piper. Maybe even the same age.

Bridget mumbled something into the wooden desk.

"Can you repeat that Ms. Monroe? Louder for the microphone."

She lifted her head, her face red and wet. She wiped her nose with her sleeve, leaving a trail of snot, "I finally realized the connection this morning. I woke up to a small pink package inside my front door: it had been slid through the mail slot. After I opened it... after I saw that poor child's picture in the news, only then did I realize the murders were connected to my bracelet." Bridget looked down, ashamed. "I'm so sorry," her voice was shaking. "I'm so, so sorry."

She was asking for forgiveness, but not from me. She needed forgiveness from someone with more power to heal than I had.

I glanced down at the note that lay on my desk in a clear evidence bag, the words scrawled in red ink: "Why won't you love me?"

We sat in silence for a moment.

"And that's why you're here. Because you connected the murders with the charms."

She sniffed, fresh tears flowing down her face. I looked at the yellowish smear of snot on her right sleeve, stretched out over the cloth like a burst bubble of gum sticking to the bottom of someone's chin. "Marcus has been out every night this week. We usually go to dinner or a movie every few days, but he keeps saying he's busy."

"And you think he knows you like Nate and will target him tonight?"

She looked up at me, her eyes fierce with earnesty, the brevity of the situation hanging heavy in the air, "Nate's a drummer."

My office door opened and Detective Lancer came in. He closed the door solemnly behind him and looked at Bridget, his face tight with bad news. The breath caught in my throat as Bridget began to shake her head, already preparing for what he was going to say.

"I'm sorry Ms. Monroe, but we were too late."

A choked sob escaped her throat and she dropped her head into her hands.

Lancer looked at me and continued, "We found the body at the music store on High St. It was officer Rodriguez's hunch. His kid takes guitar lessons there. He says it's one of the only places with practice space for bands in the area." He handed me a photo of the crime scene. A young man with brown hair was draped over the drumset, his face against one of the drums. The end of something wooden stuck out of his neck at a jarring angle. I looked closer. A drumstick had been forced through his jugular, exiting at the back of his neck. "The room was being rented by a band called The Rivals."

A noise broke from Bridget that was part sob, part scream.

Lancer passed me an evidence bag, "We found this note on the body."

I looked down at it and shuddered.

"We talked to the owner of the studio—who is understandably freaked out—and he said the victim's been taking lessons from one of the band members for months."

I looked up from the note, "Sorry?"

"I guess the victim was practicing every night this week by himself. Something about learning how to drum as a Christmas gift. Said the guy's girlfriend had a thing for musicians."

Bridget stopped crying. She raised her head slowly, wide eyes looking at me with horror. We stared at each other as Lancer continued, shaking his head sadly, "Poor guy. What we do for love."

"The murderer…" I started.

Lancer shook his head, "We think it was the drummer, the guy giving him lessons. He was long gone when we got there. We've got cars out looking for him now."

I looked back down at the evidence bag in my hands. I recognized the handwriting from the other notes. This message was written in the same bright red ink:

Merry Christmas, my love. Now we can be together. Forever.

Salt

The four of us walked down the deserted street. Wallace, Kim, Roger, and I. It was 4:00 am and we had finally grown tired of the bars. We had been celebrating Kim and Roger's marriage, the reception was long over but the four of us were still going strong. We were walking to nowhere in particular, still wearing our wedding attire and reveling in drunken intimacy. The balmy Louisiana air felt delicious against my skin, even in mid-December.

The blackness of the sky was comforting, draping around us like a velvet blanket. The yellow globes of the streetlamps held it up, keeping it from falling and suffocating us. It reminded me of when I used to read under the covers as a child, my knees acting as tent poles while I held my flashlight between my shoulder and my jawbone. A mystery novel engrossing me so much I didn't register the discomfort.

Even now, 60 years after that night, I feel the pain in my jaw. Not the pain of a full life but the pain of my decaying body. Arthritis creeps through my bones like frozen tendrils, leather whips that wrap tight around each joint. Squeezing and squeezing, leaving me stiff. A prisoner in my own body.

I'm sorry. I seem to have gotten a bit flowery with age. As if these similes and metaphors could keep death at bay. Distract the bastard long enough for me to have a few more agonizing moments of life.

There I go again.

We walked down the deserted street.

"I think it's snowing," Kim whispered, awestruck.

The four of us stopped our trek. I looked up to see small white flakes drifting lazily around us.

"That's impossible." My voice was quiet, meeting the soft reverence of Kim's tone. We rarely got snow this far south.

I tilted my head back and stuck out my tongue. A small flake danced down from the heavens to land on it, dissolving at the gentle touch.

I looked in shock at Kim, who was mimicking my behavior. "It's salt."

Wallace raised an eyebrow at me before cupping his hand out in front of him. White flakes began to collect in his palm, but they did not melt at his touch.

"What on earth…?" Roger asked the sky.

"Guys," Wallace said and I looked towards where he gestured.

In front of us, the salt was beginning to collect. Within seconds thousands of particles had gathered into the form of two feet, then two legs. A torso, arms, and neck followed. And then, before us, stood a man. A large man made entirely of salt. His salt eyes stared at nothing, yet I could feel his gaze on my skin, and my arms prickled with goosebumps.

He beckoned to us. I turned to Wallace, who stood motionless, his eyes wide with shock and incomprehension. He swallowed and stepped backward, shaking his head and I looked back to the salt man.

He was upon us, mere inches from me. I opened my mouth to scream. He grabbed my wrist and everything immediately went black.

I awoke to a dull whiteness. I blinked, trying to clear my vision before realizing that there was nothing to clear. I was in a large white room, dimly lit with white light. The walls arched high above our heads. I looked down and saw that I was lying in loose white powder. My nostrils stung and I sat up, brushing the loose salt from my bare arms. My green bridesmaid dress looked stained in the faint light.

I looked back up and realization hit me with horror. The old salt mines. They ran under the rural part of town like a maze. Our family owned large shares of the mining company, so our fathers brought us down on tours a few times to see our heritage.

I reached and touched the earthy white wall beside me, the hard substance beneath my hand rough. The air inside the mines was heavy and dry, sucking at the moisture inside my skin, my body. Draining me slowly.

The room was lit by an unnatural white glow. The salt man stood in front of us, emanating the supernatural luminescence.

A hand grasped mine and I looked down to see Kim's thin hand. Our grandmother's emerald wedding band washed out in the white light. I squeezed and she squeezed back, just like when we were little. Cousins in blood, but sisters in spirit.

The salt man turned and began to walk deeper into the mine. As he left, his light followed him and the room around us grew dark. A darkness so complete, so black, that it threatened to suffocate me. I stood frantically, dropping Kim's hand, and stumbled forward, following the man and his light in desperation.

I could hear heavy, unsure movement as Kim, Wallace, and Roger stood and followed.

We followed the man in silence through several white tunnels. The ground was at a slight decline and we went deeper and deeper into the earth. The ceilings grew lower and I had to crouch.

After what felt like hours, we stopped outside a small cavern. I held my heels in one hand, having taken them off miles before. My expensive stockings were torn and soiled from sweat and salt. My throat stung and I was in desperate need of water, my tongue large, tacky, and stiff. I tried to swallow but felt no relief.

Inside the cavern was a chest, the wood warped and rotten. A heavy black lock hung at the front, long rusted.

I was pushed aside and Wallace stepped forward into the room, Roger behind him. I looked at Kim, who looked as bad as I felt. The bottom of her wedding dress was tattered, the delicate lace falling from the skirt. Her once sparkling white dress now dark and tarnished, like the walls of salt around us. She reached a hand out towards me and I grabbed it.

Wallace knelt in front of the chest. The salt man stood to the side, watching.

"It looks old," said Wallace, who always had a knack for stating the obvious. He pulled at the lock once, testing its strength, then again harder. It came apart with a rusty crunch. Wallace twisted the once heavy lock and tossed it on the ground beside him.

The lid of the chest opened with a dry crack. I expected the insides to glow, but instead, the gold bars appeared dull and red in spots.

Roger pushed Wallace aside and reached into the chest, grabbing one of the bars. He examined it. "These are stamped with the Royal seal, they're from Britain. How'd they end up here?"

"Pirates," Kim whispered, her eyes wide, staring at the salt man Wallace and Roger seemed to have forgotten about.

I shook my head at her. There was a rumor in our family that part of our great grandfather's wealth had been stolen by pirates, but it was just that -- a rumor.

The salt man opened his mouth in a wide, toothless grin, before grabbing Wallace by the back of the neck.

Wallace cried out in surprise, his voice close and hollow in the small chamber. The salt man pushed his head into the rotten chest, the wood cracking under the force. He brought his head up and I looked with horror at Wallace's face, broken and bloodied. His right eye was closed and his other eye looked at me, begging for help.

The salt man brought his head down, again and again, the cracks turning wet as Wallace's blood exploded against the dull white walls. The salt man himself was stained pink and soon, Wallace's cries died to nothing.

Roger, mouth agape, still holding the gold bar, stared at the salt man. I turned and began to run, trying to lead Kim by the hand down the salt tunnels behind us. She dug her feet and resisted.

"Roger!" she cried. He turned to look at her, then down at the gold bar. He nodded, absentmindedly, before reaching towards the chest for another. "Come on, Roger!" his new wife screamed, her voice wet with phlegm and fear.

His hand reached around another bar as the salt man dropped Wallace's lifeless body to the ground. I pulled harder on Kim, forcing her further down the tunnel, as she reached for Roger.

He turned and started to leap from the room when the salt man's hand grabbed him.

Kim's scream filled the mines and I tripped with the sudden force of her stop. Her hand slid from mine as I fell, the hard salt grinding against my face like sandpaper. I sucked in air sharply as the salt seeped into the fresh wound, stinging like wasps.

I turned back to see Kim banging at the salt man's chest as he held Roger up by the neck with one hand. The other hand came up and grabbed Kim's left wrist, holding it up so that even I could see the emerald wedding band shine in the supernatural light of the ghostly pirate.

He howled, the sound of sand through a rain stick, thunder and anger. He squeezed and I heard the crack of Roger's neck as he went limp. He fell to the floor like Wallace had, his friend's blood, which covered the room, pooling around him as if it were his own.

Kim, face red and wet, reached for his body screaming. The salt man lifted her wrist higher, keeping her close to him. He brought his now free hand over her ring finger.

I inhaled, the thick cloying air around me tinged with the coppery smell of blood and got to my knees. I dragged myself forward and then hesitated. I looked from Kim, my cousin by blood, my sister by choice, and then to the salt man who held her in his grasp, wrestling her wedding ring from her finger.

Kim's wedding dress was ripped and stained with salt, sweat, tears, and blood. She pulled feebly against the salt man, but it was obvious she was no match.

I hesitated, debating what to do as I watched them struggle. Then I turned and fled. Kim's cries of pain and fear followed me for several turns before fading to nothing. I would stop from time to time, listening for any sounds, but never heard anything but my own heavy breathing.

I was in the mines for many hours before I found an active tunnel. By the time I was above ground again, it was late evening and I spent the night in the hospital as the doctors treated my severe dehydration and shock. I tried to explain but no one believed me. They assumed we got drunk and snuck down into the mines for fun. We got lost and I was the only one who was able to find my way again.

No one ever found Kim or the bodies of Wallace and Roger.

Eventually, the memories of that night became distant and faded. Till one day, years ago.

I went into my ensuite restroom to freshen up before breakfast and as I turned the faucet handle, all I heard was a dull roar, like sand falling, before white salt poured into the basin.

It fell for several seconds before it stopped. Resting on the pile was my grandmother's emerald wedding ring.

And with that, my brief story has ended. I wish there was more to tell. Unfortunate, really. Despite the arthritis and the pain, I want to live. But he has finally come for me. He still does not speak but yet, I understand. He is giving me time to write my story, and then my time will have come to an end. My last word will be my last breath.

My hands are heavy on the keys. Grandmother's emerald band shines on my right middle finger. I never married, but I kept the ring. A reminder of family, of love, of promises, of blood.

I know now why the pirate let me keep my years, let me live my life for all this time. I feel the dehydration from that night again, my saliva and blood beginning to run dry. The salt man knows this tale is almost over, and so he has begun to take that which he claimed all those years ago. My fingertips are white. At first I thought it was callouses, but then I recognized that particular earthy hue. That particular natural white. The white of salt deep in the mines.

I can feel my blood crystalizing, can feel my cheeks absorb my tears.

My life was not a fun one, but it was mine and he let me live it. I do not wish to lose it, even now when my body aches and my fingers struggle to type as my joints stiffen. He bought me with years, sparing me then so he could fully take me now.

But I do not want to go. I do not want to die and join him deep in the mines, his tomb. Even now, as each breath burns and my mouth puckers with the brining of my own flesh, I want to stay.

But that is the nature of the world, is it not? To breathe and to die. To consume and to be consumed. Our lives revolve around it. Breath and death, both constant and eternal.

As ubiquitous as salt.

I was a Christmas Elf

TW: See Trigger Warning Appendix

Mrs. Claus sat in her rocker, a half-completed sweater resting on her lap. The alarm clock on the small table beside her rang its shrill alarm through the warm air of the house, announcing that it was now 1 am. She reached for it, hitting the button at the top with a light ting and silencing the sound. She cranked the dial back another hour so that it would ring at 2 am.

This was how we kept track of Santa's journey on Christmas Eve.

"How are those cookies looking?"

Chandrelle opened the oven door and peered inside. "The chocolate chip cookies need another few minutes," she stood and looked at the counter behind her, touching a finger to one of the cooling gingerbread men, "but the gingerbread men are ready for decoration!"

I looked up from my piping, "The sugar cookies are almost done too!"

Mrs. Claus beamed at us before continuing her knitting, "Good, good! You girls are such good little elves."

The kitchen counters were covered with cooling racks of sugar cookies decorated with red and green frosting, pinwheel cookies with chocolate and coconut layers, and almond shortbread cookies dusted with powdered sugar. Several pies cooled in the window, the chilled glass absorbing their heat to create a moist fog that blurred the snowy wonderland outside. I had made apple and pumpkin pies as well as some meat pies with the beef leftover from the cows we had in the summer.

Meat pie wasn't something we normally had at the Christmas feast, but it had been Horith's favorite and I wanted to honor him. To feel like he was still included in the celebration. My heart stung at his memory and my eyes watered. I wanted to fall to the floor and cry, but it was Christmas and I had to put on a happy face for the younger elves. I swallowed my pain down and forced myself to smile as I worked. I would be able to cry later in the quiet safety of the barn, away from the observant eyes of Mr. and Mrs. Claus.

Once the cookies were finished baking, Chandrelle started to roast the Christmas ham. The boys, who were now busying themselves with the stables, had slaughtered the pig earlier that week. Fresh potatoes and corn harvested at the end of the fall and root vegetables from the cellar would complete the feast.

Santa always came back on Christmas hungry, even after eating the treats left by little boys and girls all around the world. Once he returned, we'd all celebrate the success of the holiday with him. It would be joyful to have everyone enjoy the sweet and savory treats created by me and Chandrelle.

This year there were twelve of us elves. Chandrelle and I were the eldest. At nineteen, Chandrelle was the oldest elf I had ever known. I had always joked that it was her baking skills that kept her alive so long.

I was the second eldest at sixteen. Until Thanksgiving, it had been Horith who was the second eldest. He had been seventeen. Horith and I had been very close. Our love ran deep and constant like the river that bordered the North Pole on the south side.

Being one of the two eldest female elves came with a lot of privileges and responsibilities. We were not only expected to take care of the younger elves but to help Mrs. Claus with running the house, which meant also the barn and the cellar. We were the only ones that she would entrust to protect the food storages since some of the younger elves would be less able to fight temptation during times when food was scarce.

After Chandrelle and me was Myrin who was fourteen. Then there was Erolith who had just turned twelve and Zaltarish who was eleven. Cystenn was nine, the twins Arazorwyn and Biafyndar were eight, Pleufan was seven, and Alok was four. Then there was sweet Quaeth, who was the second youngest at one year old.

And finally, there was precious little Nym, who was only six months. She was to spend the holiday tucked tightly in her crib, drunk on breast milk and dreaming of sugar plums.

I had a special bond with Nym because she was the first elf harvested from me. After years of fearing that I wouldn't be able to contribute new elves to the Pole, Nym finally came along. My little miracle. When Santa had punished Horith I worried he would take his anger out on Nym as well. I begged him to spare her, that it was only me who was a threat to the joyful life at the North Pole.

I will always be thankful to Mrs. Claus for saving our lives that night, even if her motives were only driven by concern for our small number. Her frantic cries warned Santa that losing two adult elves would be unwise in the harsh winter months and even losing one infant would make the future difficult.

At Mrs. Claus' pleading, he decided to show us both mercy that day, only locking us in the shed for a week as penance for my failings.

See, the North Pole is a wonderful land of celebration and joy, but also of discipline and reverence. We elves have few rules we must follow, but disobedience is not an option.

Rule #1: Do your chores.

The eldest female elves looked after the home and the food reserves in the barn and cellar. We baked, cooked, pickled, cleaned, and did all the sewing. The eldest male elves looked after the animals and performed the butchering. Sometimes, under Santa's supervision, the boys would be allowed to travel north towards the mountains to hunt rabbits and deer. Chandrelle had always envied their trips away. Neither of us had ever traveled past the tree line.

Horith would tell me all about the animals and the views that he saw during those trips. We'd sneak to the barn late at night and lie together in the hay. He'd tell me about how rocky and steep the mountains grew as you approached them and how beautiful the sun was setting over the Pole.

After their tenth year, elves were expected to help look after the crops and contribute to the harvests. It was tough work for such small bodies, but we all had to do our part. Horith had been so good about helping the little ones with their more difficult chores after he had finished all of his. When they weren't in the fields, they either took care of the younger elves or assisted the older elves in more detailed tasks. This also helped them learn the jobs that they would soon be expected to perform. The youngest elves were in charge of the easier chores, such as taking care of the chickens and collecting eggs or helping with the gardening.

When all the elves did their chores, the North Pole ran smoothly. Like a well-oiled machine. Even this past year with only twelve of us, we were all able to survive. And it was indeed lucky that Chandrelle and Myrin were both ripe with the next generation of elves, promising that our numbers would grow again.

Rule #2: Always be joyful.

Mrs. Claus told us that a smile is all you need in this world. That it is a conduit for joy. When we felt bad things she'd shush us.

"Santa does not like it when elves cry," she'd warn.

But sometimes it was hard, especially for the little ones. We'd remind them to try and be joyful even when they had stubbed their toe or skinned their knee, but still the tears would flow around their frowns. We'd tell them that it'd get easier as they grew older. They'd sniffle and nod and we'd smile at them, rewarding their joy with cookies and candy.

What I never revealed was that it was difficult to be joyful, even as an older elf, and so I had to pretend. When Mr. Claus could see my unjoyfulness seeping through my smiling face, he'd tell me to be more like the other elf girls. To be more like Chandrelle or Mrs. Claus, whose warm smile never faltered. Mrs. Claus with those ice-blue eyes, crinkled permanently by a wide toothy smile.

Mr. and Mrs. Claus said that elves were always joyful, so I used to worry that I was defective. But then I started going to the barn at night with Horith and he told me that he wasn't joyful either.

Rule #3: Only Santa may leave the Pole.

The only exception being when he would take the older boys hunting. Otherwise, only Santa was able to come and go. And he didn't leave only on Christmas Eve but would leave the Pole once or twice a month. I once asked Mrs. Claus what

Santa did when he left and she explained that he needed things that we couldn't provide at the North Pole.

Despite her unfaltering smile, she'd sympathize with us, the girl elves, on those nights. These were the nights when Santa would visit us in our room. Most of us wouldn't be able to sleep those nights, not when we knew what was coming. He'd waken the few that could early in the morning, our thin door banging against the wall.

The sound would always vibrate through my bones as a sour scent permeated the room, making the warm air heavy over my mouth, forever forced into a smile.

He'd pick one or two of the girl elves and carry us out to the shed where he would ready us for harvesting new elves. It wasn't at all like when Horith and I would go to the barn. That would be soft and painless. It hurt when Santa sowed us.

I was lucky though. Chandrelle was his favorite, so I was often left alone.

There was an unspoken fourth rule at the Pole: that only Santa may harvest his elves. We were supposed to be pure. But Horith and I loved each other. We loved each other so much that our bodies ached to be together.

And then Mr. Claus found us.

He had been so proud of me too. So proud that I had finally provided fruit for him and Mrs. Claus. It was then that he took Horith to the shed. That was the last time I saw my love, his face twisted in fear and pain as Santa dragged him through the cold dead leaves. I cried for him, openly. Mrs. Claus allowed it, even though it was not joy. She had always been much kinder than Santa.

The alarm rang at 6 am. Mrs. Claus stopped her knitting and stood at the window, looking out at the winter landscape around us. Worry furrowed her brow, slightly wrinkling her otherwise joyful face. Santa Claus had never been this late getting home before.

At 11 am, Mrs. Claus let us eat some of the feast that we had prepared so that we could go to bed without empty stomachs. I couldn't sleep though, instead, I listened to her walk back and forth by the front windows, waiting for him.

At 3 pm, the other girl elves and I joined her in the living room. At this point, she was curled up on her rocking chair. She wasn't crying, which I was surprised by. Despite Rule #2, I understood the hurt that happens when someone you love doesn't come back. Yet instead, Mrs. Claus rocked back and forth, her eyes glazed, staring out into nothing. She was unresponsive. Her lips drawn tight, making her grin look dehydrated and skeletal.

By the time 5 pm hit we abandoned her to feed the younger elves more of the Christmas feast which now lay cold on the table.

At 8 pm, Chandrelle called out for me to join her at the window. I hugged Nym close to my chest as I walked over to see. Chandrelle pointed and I immediately saw the shadowy figure which had just emerged from the treeline. Mrs. Claus jumped from her chair, pushing us aside to take a look.

"Oh thank God! He's back!" She cried, the practiced smile of joy stretching her face wide again. We continued to look over her shoulder as another shadowy figure appeared, followed by another. Soon, several shadows were walking towards the house.

Mrs. Claus' face went pale and, for the first time, her smile wavered. It felt as if ice water was running down my spine. She ran to the back of the house and came barreling back moments later with a large shotgun. She brandished the weapon in front of her as she ran out the door wearing nothing but her housecoat and slippers.

There was a loud bang and she fell into the snow, which quickly turned red around her.

We were too stunned to react. Within seconds strange men were around us, touching us and asking us questions in short barks. Chandrelle smiled widely at them, asking if they wanted some cookies and Christmas cheer.

Nym and I were the only ones who cried.

I haven't seen any of the other elves since. The men let me keep Nym though, which I appreciate. They gave me a cup of water and a cup of some warm brown liquid I assumed was Hot Cocoa, but it was bitter and earthy. I spit it out and the men took it away.

They asked me lots of questions, many of which I didn't understand. It was like they were speaking a different language. They asked me who my mother and father are, but I don't know what those words mean.

I asked if I could go back to the North Pole, but the men only clenched their jaws without answering. Their features were sharp and their flesh was not snowy white. They were not elves. They all looked different, it was difficult to keep them straight. They were all odd-looking. And each of them looked old. Much older than Mrs. Claus. They looked like they were Santa's age.

I am alone now. This place is too bright, too cold, too metallic. The light hurts my eyes and the coldness gnaws at my bones. Tears bite at my cheeks. I try to smile but it is hard to even pretend to feel joy here.

The warmth of Nym on my chest is the only comfort I have. She squirms and I look down at her and try again to smile. She looks up at me and her large wet eyes search my features before lighting up with recognition. She smiles at me and my heart lightens. I see Horith's smile in hers and for the first time since he died, my smile feels real.

Spiders in the Chimney

In the fall of my ninth birthday, my family moved from a small two-bedroom apartment to a six-bedroom farmhouse. We hadn't lived in a city necessarily, more like a big town, but compared to the country surrounding the farmhouse it might as well have been New York City. The house wasn't exactly in the best shape: shingles hung loosely from the roof like crooked teeth, the shutters were missing several grey—once black—slats, and the red paint on the vinyl siding was being eaten away by age and disrepair.

Despite my parents referring to the house as a farmhouse my whole life, I've realized as an adult that the building is surprisingly modern for the year it was built. Having stood at least through the seventies if not before, the house's slanted roof started low on the left side and ended touching the sky on the right.

Bay windows topped with abstract stained glass filled the high walls on the right, softening the angles of the house. The right wall ended in a steepled tower sticking out from the roof. A small window was recessed into the tower. My heart fluttered with excitement the first time I saw it. I knew before even stepping foot into our new home that the tower would be my room.

Mom explained that we moved for my dad. The farmhouse came with a large barn that he planned to repurpose as a workshop. Construction site supervisor by day, woodworker by night, my dad's dream had always been to have his own workshop and make woodworking his full-time job. When we didn't have the space, woodworking was just a passion, a well-loved hobby that took my dad across the river to a mill-turned-studio-space a few nights a week. We had only lived in the farmhouse for a few months before the barn had been transformed into a woodworker's paradise.

The farmhouse was huge. The first floor consisted of a kitchen, pantry, a large spacious living room, dining room, and a sunroom off the back. I did not spend much time on that floor the first day. Instead, I spent the first hour drifting frantically from one bedroom to the next, searching for the room which was to become my own.

The second floor of the house was half-open space and half bedrooms. The hallway, instead of lined with two walls, was lined with doors to the rooms on one side and a railing overlooking the living room on the other. Standing at the railing gave you an all-encompassing view of the living room while the slanted ceiling hung low over your head.

I ran from room to room in glee, standing in the middle of each, inhaling the dusty air deeply, then running out in a burst of excitement to see the next. None of the four rooms on the second floor were satisfactory, so I ran up the creaking wooden steps to the third floor. The third floor was smaller than the second floor, the ceiling cutting into it so that it only took up half the width of the house. I explored the two large rooms set on opposite sides of the hall, identical to each other, both dirty with disuse. I left the twin rooms in haste, knowing that

I had been prolonging the discovery of my bedroom, drawing out the inevitable exploration of the tower.

My expedition brought me to the far side of the thin hallway, which ended in a small white door. I opened it without caution and was rewarded with a narrow staircase. Thick layers of cobwebs traced the corners of the stairs, worn from footfalls over the years which had created shallow divots in the middle of each step.

My enthusiasm waned as I looked up into the darkness, which was complete and suffocating. I searched the wall beside me for a light switch but there was none. I steadied myself and took one hesitant step up into the black.

The steps groaned beneath my weight as I took each with a deliberate determination. My vision began to fade into shadow but as I crept to the top of the stairs, I noticed a slight light. I brought my foot up and almost fell with surprise at the lack of another step—I was at the top.

I turned to the small window, the source of the faint light, and walked towards it. Small shutters were locked in place by a small silver hook. I lifted the hook and threw the shutters back with a loud bang, bathing the room in muted sunlight.

The tower room was small, about ten feet across. The walls were entirely round, surrounding me in a perfect circle cut along the far wall by three feet of brick wall that jutted out into the space. The brick continued up past the ceiling - the chimney, I realized. Examining the space in the light, I could now see a small ledge about three feet high and two feet wide cut into the wall next to the stairs, partially blocked by the wooden railing.

My heart fluttered with the tickle of love at first sight. I ran down the stairs, skipping steps in my excitement to tell my mom and dad that I had found my new bedroom.

Within a week, my tower had been cleaned and my mom had painted the walls a dark blue. Small white circles dotted the ceiling, making up constellations of stars. We hung white Christmas lights to give my dark room a warm glow. The back of my white metal bed frame rested against the brick chimney, which allowed my bed to be flat against the otherwise curved wall. I filled the nook in the staircase with stuffed animals and action figures. A tall bookcase and dresser along with a small desk and chair completed the room.

I remember snuggling between the fresh sheets, perfectly at peace with my new home. As my mind drifted to sleep, I could hear a small rustling coming from the chimney behind me.

November descended on the farmhouse and a cold draft began to manifest against the thin walls, tendrils of the wintry chill outside sneaky soundlessly towards the warm insides of the house. On the first frigid night, Dad tried to light a fire in the living room fireplace. The flames grew quickly, reaching high into the chimney as the downstairs quickly filled with a noxious black cloud. Mom threw every window open wide as my dad took me out onto the front yard and then ran back in. The image of black smoke pouring from the windows of the farmhouse - still looking old and worn while my parents worked to repair it - was terrifying yet beautiful. The black smoke looked evil and dangerous but the contrast of it against the red and flaking walls of the house was striking, leaving a lasting impression on my young mind.

My parents soon got the smoke under control and I was led back into the house, which now smelled like burnt toast.

"Chimney must be blocked," my dad said matter-of-factly, "I'll have to clean it out."

"Or pay an expert to do it," my mom suggested. My dad shrugged at her.

The fire had stirred something inside the chimney. The small rustling I had gotten used to hearing at night grew louder, almost as if distressed. I was unnerved by the sound but I restrained myself from running to my parents' room. My dad had warned me that I was getting too old to sleep with them. I wanted to prove to him that I was a big boy, that I could sleep in my own room. But the noise was chilling, like the rustling of paper. Chittering and skittering, the sound of a muffled maraca.

The sound reminded me of the rainstick Mrs. Paxon, my teacher, had brought into class once. She turned it one way and then the other, the cooling hiss of sand running over nails and wood creating ghostly tingles at the back of my neck. But it was menacing, like a stampede in the distance, the combined force of hundreds of animals unaware of the damage caused by the combined power of their hooved feet.

One Saturday morning, over pancakes with maple syrup and thick strips of fatty bacon, I told my father that there was a ghost living in the chimney and I could hear him moving at night.

His laugh was hearty and warm, "It's probably just mice," he said over mouthfuls of sticky pancake, "I bet their nest is what's blocking the damn chimney."

I shook my head stubbornly. When we first moved in there were mice in the barn. Dad bought traps and I cried because he was going to kill them. He ended up buying non-lethal mouse traps and releasing the ones he caught far from the house. But in the process, I had learned what mice sound like and whatever was in the chimney was not mice.

"There's no squeaking. And it sounds like a lot of something. If it is mice, there must be hundreds!" I exclaimed dramatically.

My father laughed again, "Alright, alright. Calm yourself, Jacob. I'll check after breakfast."

Once the pancakes and bacon had been eaten and the coffee and orange juice finished, my dad and I went to the fireplace. Dad knelt down on his knees and shone a flashlight up towards the top of the chimney. He moved the beam of light this way and that, his eyes squinting.

"There's definitely something up there," he craned his neck further, "What the…" he said as his light caught the culprit.

Suddenly, my father jumped backward, banging his head hard against the brick opening. "Ah, fuck!" he cried, falling onto the living room floor. I stepped back in surprise: my father never swore. "Jesus fucking Christ!" he yelled, scooting away from the fireplace in absolute horror.

My mom ran in from the kitchen, "What is it? What's wrong?" she asked, her face strained with worry.

Dad stood up, roughly wiping at his sleeves and front as if rubbing burning embers from his shirt. He looked up at her, his teeth bared, "Goddamn spiders!" He seethed, "the bloody chimneys full of them!"

They stared at each other, my mom's mouth slightly agape, my father's body rising and falling with his angry breath.

The silence was broken with my mother's warm laughter.

"Dammit, Margaret! This isn't funny!" my dad said, which made my mother laugh even harder. She bent over herself, clutching her stomach. Wiping tears from her eyes, her laughter finally settled and she looked up at my dad. Two hundred and twenty pounds of muscle and bone, hard work and calluses. Brine, vinegar, and salt.

That was the day I discovered the only thing my father feared beyond losing me and my mother were spiders.

"Want me to squash them for you?" my mother chided.

"It's not funny," there was a hint of embarrassment in his voice, "the bastards are huge. Wolf spiders probably." He shivered and my mom smiled at him as she rubbed his arm.

"We'll call someone in to take care of them."

"We don't have the money," my father said in a hushed tone.

"Well," my mother's voice was loud as if to compensate for his whisper, "in the meantime, they haven't done anything to us yet other than block our chimney, so I think we'll survive for another week or so until we've got the funds." She wrapped an arm around my father, his pride wounded, "and please stop swearing in front of Jacob."

Dad grunted at her. He glared threateningly at a floorboard as if it had personally affronted him.

A few weeks later and the spiders remained in our chimney. Dad didn't seem to be selling his woodwork as much as he thought he would and because all the construction sites were closed until the snow cleared, he couldn't get another job in the meantime. Mom was working extra shifts at the hospital but still, the spiders stayed. Unwanted roommates we couldn't kick out. But I guess it had been their house first.

At night, I'd hear their hairy paws scuttering across the bare bricks by my head and I'd hug my teddy bear tight. Dad had gone from the first floor to my tower, filling any holes in the bricks with foam insulation to keep them contained.

We'd often forget about our creepy housemates, however, and in those moments the place felt warm and loving. Dad had gotten the oil heater in the basement running again and so dry heat emanated from the radiators throughout the house. Mom fixed up two of the rooms as guest rooms for when family and friends visited, one as a playroom for me, and the last room as a computer room. The old and forgotten house quickly morphed into an inviting home.

Our first Christmas in the farmhouse was an exciting one. Mom had gone all out decorating: illuminated pine garlands hung from every railing and mantle, lined with candy canes. Red and green striped stockings hung above the fireplace and candles sat in every one of the many windows. Our Christmas tree towered in the open living room, its star only a foot below the tall ceiling.

I curled up into bed on Christmas Eve, my skin crackling with the excitement of the coming day.

I awoke suddenly. The room was dark but moonlight streamed through the small window across from me, illuminating everything with a silver glow. My heart was racing and I could hear my blood flowing through my veins, filling my ears with a low rumble.

Something had woken me up. Something was wrong.

My body was stiff with fear as I strained my ears, trying to hear what had woken me.

"Ho… ho… ho…." a voice creaked.

I no longer believed in Santa but even if I did, I knew that voice was wrong. It was not the voice of a friend. It was the voice of an intruder, dry and cracked. A voice echoing through forgotten crevices, etched with time and hate.

"Ho… ho… ho…" the voice creaked again, this time louder, closer to my face.

My heart stopped, my breath caught in my throat.

"Ho… ho… ho…" With a boom, my heart pounded loudly and I stifled my cry. The voice was coming from inside the chimney. I hugged my bear to my chest, pursing my lips tight together to prevent the whimpers from escaping my mouth.

"Ho… ho… ho…" the voice said again, this time below my bed. Whatever it was, it was moving downwards.

44

The fireplace.

I sat up slowly, still clinging to my teddy bear, and softly placed my feet beside my bed. I stood.

"Ho… ho… ho…" It was fainter now.

As quietly as I could, I padded down the stairs. I was beginning to know those steps. To know where the sensitive spots were that would scream if you stepped on them. My socked feet traced the edges, making only the softest murmur against the wood.

At the third floor, I stood in the doorway of the computer room below my tower and listened.

"Ho… ho… ho…" The voice was getting louder. Not closer, but louder, as if the one emitting it was getting more invested in the holiday spirit.

I followed it down to the first floor. The door to my parent's bedroom opened with a small creak and I jumped. My father's concerned face appeared. He looked down, saw me, and stepped out before placing a protective hand on my shoulder. I saw his shotgun in his other hand.

I had seen the shotgun for the first time a few months beforehand, during fall when my father set out to hunt our Thanksgiving turkey. It was a yearly tradition but, before the farmhouse, the gun would remain locked in dad's studio. Now it lived in a locked box at the top of my parent's bedroom closet.

"Ho… ho… ho…" the raspy voice grated through the air sending chills down my spine.

Dad looked down and placed a finger to his lip in a gesture of silence. I nodded. He turned away from me and began to climb down the stairs. I followed a ways behind, my confidence rising with the presence of my father and his gun to protect me.

We followed the voice down to the living room, which glowed with the soft lights hanging from the Christmas tree.

"Ho… ho… ho…" the voice trickled through the opening of the fireplace, echoing along the brick walls, magnifying till it reached out towards us, grasping for us. My father towered in the middle of the room as I cowered behind the couch, peeking over the back.

A black shape slowly emerged from the fireplace. My dad raised the shotgun to his shoulder. The shape came forward and landed on the wooden floor with a soft click.

We stared at the shape, unable to recognize it. It was thick and long, jointed and knobby like a stick, but the surface was smooth and shiny and black. It stretched out into the living room but the other end was still unseen, hidden deep inside the chimney. Whatever we were seeing was only part of it.

"Ho… ho… ho…" the voice was almost upon us, hanging heavy in the air like a thick fog. I shuddered with the cold that emanated from the fireplace. From the thing inside.

Another black shape, identical to the first, slithered out. My father took a step back, his gun swinging from one shape to the other.

A black mass lowered down from the chimney, so large it completely filled the fireplace. The black was so complete, so deep that it seemed like we were staring at nothing at all.

The first shiny black shape rose into the air and landed a foot in front of where it had been, the other following, the black mass growing, as if being pulled forward. Another two of the shapes emerged from the fireplace to join their brothers.

Legs. They were legs, I realized. A scream caught in my throat.

My father seemed to realize as well because he ran to the couch, grabbed me, and pushed me to the stairs.

46

"Run. Go to your mother," he said. He turned without checking that I obeyed his orders and lifted the gun again.

I ran up the stairs, looking behind me as I did. The black mass flowed from the fireplace like thick molten lava, growing slowly but containing the power to destroy anything in its path. I turned the corner of the stairs, reached the top, and ran to the railing overlooking the living room.

The mass slid out completely, followed by another large shadow being vomited forth from our hearth. Two more legs appeared and then the rest of the beast fell and rose, no longer constrained by its brick prison.

A giant monster, deformed into a grotesque mimicry of a spider, towered over my father. Its abdomen was the size of a large dog, covered in coarse hair, red like old rust. Two pointed needles stuck out from the bottom, snow-white strings coming out from between them. The spider's spinnerets pulsed as the string slackened slightly. The threads of silk gooey, like a melted marshmallow pulled apart, stretching and sticking to everything as the creature stepped forward.

The front section, the cephalothorax, hung in front of the large round abdomen, like it does for a black widow. But it was not the rounded square of a normal spider. Instead, the flat body was replaced with the torso of a very obese man. Shirtless, its thick gut hung over the top of its abdomen. What I could see of the chest was covered in rough white hair, thick and curly, coiled tightly against the pale skin which was littered with brown moles. Two pink nipples, chapped and turning white around the edges, stuck out from the fur. The bulging chest was framed by thick arms, bulking with muscle and fat, the skin hanging loosely, thin and puckered like crepe paper.

At the top of the torso was the head of a man. Or, at least something man-like. The skin was moist and dewy, its rounded cheeks blotchy with red stains. Around its nose were the red and purple lines of broken blood vessels, intersecting with each other like highways on a map. A heavy long beard fell from its chin, white hair greyed with age and unwash, stained on the edges with black soot. It landed on the floor, twisting around itself.

White matted hair flowed from the top of its head and hung loosely around its shoulders. Clay, mud, and dirt caked around the edges. Two large pupil-less eyes sat in the center of its round face, staring down at my father. Four smaller eyes rested beneath those like still pools of dark water. Two more were inlaid into its temples, one of which, I realized, my bladder emptying itself in utter horror, was looking right at me. All eight eyes were pitch black and glistening with wetness, the reflections of the Christmas tree lights making them glint viciously. Warm liquid ran down my inner thigh, the stream finding its way into the band of my wool socks. I could smell the hot scent of urine rising around me.

Drool fell from two large pinchers set into the massive jaw of the beast. The fangs were inverted triangles, coming to a thin point like a tiger's claw. They were surrounded at the base with the same coarse hair that covered the abdomen, but this hair was shorter and thicker. The muscles at the base of each fang convulsed and twitched separately from each other, the pinchers moving out of sync. Large clear droplets formed and fell.

The creature straightened its legs, rising into the air, its head brushing against the top of the ceiling, his lowest set of eyes level now with mine.

"Ho… ho… ho…" it cried. Its humanesque voice filled the large space.

There was a high-pitched scream and I looked to see my mother standing in the open doorway.

It looked at her. I could smell decay and blood heavy on its breath.

She screamed again.

Its face came towards her and I heard a shot. The room illuminated with a sharp flash of light and the beast erupted in a scream. The noise was like the bow of a violin being dragged roughly the wrong way against the waxed strings. It whipped its head towards dad, lowering its shoulders. A black leg struck out with lightning speed and my father hit the wall behind him with a crack and a thud. He fell limply to the floor, his gun hitting the wood with a hollow thunk beside him.

I looked at my mother, who stood there in shock, shaking.

"Run!" I screamed, moving towards her. I grabbed her arm as I passed and she followed me.

We ran up the stairs. My shoulder slammed hard into a wall as I turned sharply around the corner, pushing myself and my mother forward onto the third floor.

Hot pain radiated through my arm. I could hear the procession of spindly legs on the landing below us. We raced towards my open bedroom door. As we approached, I turned to look behind me and saw the creature's head emerge from the other stairway. I hesitated, drawn by the hideousness and monstrosity of the thing pulling its body - something that shouldn't exist in this world - towards us.

My mom began pulling me up. I followed, tears clouding my sight, and ran into my mother's side as she stopped. I looked up at her and she picked me up, shoving me against something soft. I blinked the tears away and was faced with a stuffed elephant. I was being pushed into my nook between the wall and the stairs. I understood and began to climb over my toys. When I reached the wall, cold from the winter night beyond it, I turned and, with my mom's help, arranged the toys so they covered me as much as possible.

I saw her run up the remaining stairs and heard metal hitting wood with a loud bang.

To my right was the noise of struggling and wood snapping. I held my breath. My view was soon eclipsed by the monster. I covered my face with my hand as the white flesh of its humanoid shoulders appeared only inches from my face.

My mom screamed and I heard something bounce off the beast with a bodily thud and land on the floor with a crash.

The creature screamed again and I saw its abdomen lunged forward past my hiding spot as a red blur.

Suddenly, the room was illuminated with another flash and my ears rang. I was dazed, the world around me had grown silent, my hearing muted as if with cotton. I saw a white t-shirt emerge, cut off by the railing in front of my face, my father.

I waited but the room was still. My hearing slowly came back, like a lens coming into focus, and I could hear my mother crying softly. My father's heavy footsteps rang out as he walked the rest of the way up to my room.

"Where's Jacob?" he asked, his voice flat.

I scooted out from my nook, animals and toys falling to the stairs clumsily.

"Dad?" My voice was small, as if the experience had taken years away from me and I was just a little boy again.

My father turned towards me, his face and shirt wet with a viscous blue liquid. My mother stepped out from behind my overturned bed. I climbed the remaining stairs to the tower floor and my father picked me up into a sticky hug. My mom joined us. The three of us shook where we stood, foreign blood covering every surface, my mom's soft crying filling the empty silence.

I took a warm bath while my father and mother cleaned up the mess. I don't know what they did with that thing's body. Knowing my father, he probably took an axe to it and brought it, piece by piece, into the woods.

After my bath, my mother, now wearing jeans and a t-shirt, tucked me into her and my father's queen bed, still clean and dry, and kissed me on the forehead.

We never talked about that night. For most of my life, I had thought it had been a horrible nightmare.

Life in the farmhouse after that was uneventful. Every year, dad called an exterminator to come to the house and spray, paying careful attention to the chimney. My dad tried to get the chimney cleaned out so we could use the fireplace but no matter what we did or how many professionals we called, fires would turn to black smoke and fill the house once again with the scent of burnt toast.

I'm in college now. Last year, like most of my peers, I went back home for Christmas. My childhood bed has since been replaced with a more comfortable full-size bed, but otherwise, the room is pretty much how it was when I was a child, plus a few band posters and minus a lot of toys. I still keep my teddy bear in a special spot on my bookcase and I still fall asleep staring up at the painted stars I have long since memorized.

The rest of the house, however, has been upgraded. With the fad of artisan-crafted furniture, my dad's woodworking has become a hot commodity. He's even had a few celebrity clients. My parents have completely replaced all the old appliances with fancy high-tech gadgets. Both the roof and the red vinyl siding have been taken apart and completely replaced. The only thing that remains untouched is the old brick chimney.

The first night I was back, I woke up suddenly, as if from a nightmare. The red numbers on the clock beside my face read 12:01 AM.

My blood went cold as I heard a rustling beside my head and a soft echo of "ho… ho… ho…"

I closed my eyes tight and waited. But nothing happened. Eventually, I fell back asleep.

This year, I'm a sophomore, living in an apartment off-campus with some friends. I invited my parents to spend Christmas with me here since my roommates will be away. I've cleaned up all the empties and thrown away the old pizza boxes. While it might not be the flashiest of Christmases - my decorating skills pale compared to my mother's - at least we'll be safe.

I Thought I Heard You

"I thought I heard you in here," my grandpa says to the room. Christmases have been rough since grandma died.

As a young child, I always looked forward to Christmas at my grandparents' house. The warm smells that floated in the air: cinnamon, cloves, and ginger mixing together into a shapeless cloud around me. Just a hint of mint tinging the air with a crispness that made the warmth all that much more pleasurable. The small home was cozy and comfortable, the polished wood worn with use, brown with age, cracked and creaking from the weight of our lives. My grandpa made sure to always have a fire roaring in the cast iron fireplace, the yellow glow playing across our faces, making the presents gleam under the tree, begging to be opened, the bright green and red metallic wrapping paper pleading to be ripped by our hands. The warmth of the flames ate at my skin, dancing expertly along the line of pleasant heat and burning pain.

My mother and grandmother would cook and bake together. They'd make pies and turkey, cranberry compote and pumpkin cookies, mountains of mashed potatoes sweetened with fresh butter and thick cream, homemade caramel and green beans with shallots, mushroom gravy and sweet potatoes with coconut, coffee crumb cake and mulled wine. The air would alight with the scents of their cooking and my stomach would kick and growl with anticipation. Grandma would slip me a cookie or a candy cane, the sweet treat accompanied with a small innocent wink. I'd eat it slowly, savoring each small bite as I eyed the rest of the meal that grew, almost organically, on the counter before me, the sights and smells tickling my nostrils. Dinner time would not come soon enough, but until then, it was a sight I hungrily devoured, my eyes full, my tastebuds lacking.

My father would read me stories, epic tales of fantasy worlds where mythical beings lived in the ground and the trees. He'd change his voice with each character and gesticulate wildly with his arms, the line of vision from his eyes to the words on the page teetering with each arching movement, each brave dwarf, each cackling witch, each billowing wizard. He'd create a magical world so believable, so engrossing, that I would become utterly entranced. The smells and sounds of the house heightening my absorption, blending my mind's eye with what was directly in front of my face, making the fake world as tangible as the real one, the real world as intangible as the one my father was creating with his voice.

My grandfather would add his own power to the Christmas cheer by playing songs on the old piano in the living room. The cabin would fill to the brim with both his fast and cheerful melodies as well as the slow and brooding songs that seemed more of a warning than a celebration. The heavy ivory keys creaking as the hammer hit the tightened string, a crystal note rising quickly to the air, only to dissipate instantly above me, showering me with sound.

And every night, as I lay awake in my grandpa's office, the cushioned cot beneath my small frame, I'd pull my favorite of grandmother's quilts, the red and white one that smelt of pine and lilacs, up to my chin to protect me from the drafts and groans of the old house. And every night, Nana would come visit me. She'd share secrets with me, stories of Santa and his reindeer, of the elves and their toys, the North Pole and how, even on the chilliest of days, no one there ever gets cold.

"No one shivers at the North Pole." Her cobwebbed throat would strain with the words. Like opening the cover of an old and forgotten book, the binding cracking, the pages falling with a thud instead of a rustle, her voice would rise with a cloud of dust. "There's magic in the air," she'd whisper, "magic that keeps everyone warm, all the time. No one ages. There are no wars, no famines. It's a magical winter paradise." She'd lean close to my face, so close that only her bright eyes filled my vision. "And you can be Queen." She'd wink at me, a slow wink, as if her eyelids were heavy, heavier than they should be.

I'd smile, "I can be Mrs. Claus?"

Nana would nod, a slow and calm nod, as her thin lips turned up into a small, tight smile.

I would fall asleep with images of the North Pole in my mind, the voice of Nana flitting about my subconscious like a lost butterfly.

"I thought I heard you in here," my grandpa says to the room.

"Who do you think is there, dad?" mom asks.

Grandpa turns to her, blinking his eyes as if adjusting to a great brightness, confusion etched on his lined face. "I thought… I thought I heard your mother."

Shushing him like one would a child, my mom escorts him out of the office, one hand firmly, but gently, grasping the side of his upper arm, the other hand on his back, guiding him away from the ghost of his dead wife.

We still visit my grandpa every Christmas. Since grandma died, he's been really lonely. My mom, dad, and I always make the trek up to his cabin. My parent's old station wagon slowly dragging us up the mountain, tracing the snowy winding roads. Even with my thick winter coat and the dry heat from the dashboard, the cold creeps through the car's windows and bites at my skin like a snake.

The smells of Christmas are fainter now than they were when I was young, the rooms slightly cooler, the house less comfortable. Sometimes I'll sit in my grandma's old rocking chair and a shiver will suddenly break over my body, running from the top of my head through my neck and deep into the bottom of my spine. Whether from cold, loss, fear, or all three, I do not know.

It is now my job to stoke the fires. Grandpa is too old, too lost in the archaic crevices of his mind. He stares out the windows for too long, his eyes no longer seeing, the cold begging him to give in. Mom still cooks and bakes, but each year there is less and less food. Each year our holiday feast morphs more into a simple dinner. Instead of reading to me, dad plays sudoku on his smartphone, the blue glow illuminating his face, scrunched in calculated concentration.

I like to think back to my younger years often. The warmth of the cabin, an enveloping hug, holding me close, protecting me from the outside, from the snow. Nana sitting on the edge of my bed, whispering to me, her voice barely audible, almost too quiet to carry through the air. Each word would rise and fall with the indiscernible movements of the draft in the chilly office. Her voice was light, like a broken feather, fluttering towards me, landing lightly on my skin, tracing my features as it crawled from every direction, sliding slowly into my ears.

Images of a great man, strong and ancient, standing proudly over his workers filled my mind. His long grey beard flowing gracefully down like a waterfall, stopping in a wispy curl against the dirt ground, packed hard from years of toiling, years of heavy boots and sharp keratin hooves. His mass filling the room, the space glowing red as his body reflects in the polished stone surrounding him on all sides. Stone flat and tall like walls but bigger, higher, stretching endlessly into the black cloudless sky.

"You can barely breath at the North Pole, for he encompasses all, even the molecules of air your lungs need and the blood your veins crave."

"But Nana, won't I die if I can't breathe?"

Nana's chuckle was low and each strained sound was cut short, like a cough deep in someone's chest, muffled and painful as they try hard not to let it escape. "No, child. You won't die at the North Pole." She brought her dry, crusty lips closer to my face, "You'll live forever." Her breath, a strange mix of peppermint and mud, kissed the tip of my nose delicately, like a ballerina, weighing almost nothing, as close to air as a human could ever be.

She told me stories of the different types of elves that live at the North Pole: the ones that carry long leathery whips, stained a deep rust color that flaked, the whip strong while the stains fragile, only permanent through repeated application. The elves that had dark metal spears, the points of which were so small, they dissolved into atoms.

"The tip is so fine, one poke, and you don't even realize you've been pierced." her voice, so impossibly rough and strained.

Images danced across my mind. Pictures of elves with cutting, blood-stained knives, elves with red hot matches. Elves with heavy chains, with chisels meant to flay skin, hooks to pierce and pull at flesh, pliers, boiling water, pins and needles and thread. Elves created to pierce, burn, tear, cut, and break the bodies of the sinners. Sinners no longer in the hands of an angry god, but instead in the claws of a loving demon, so infatuated with every inch of their skin, the softness of their lips, the moistness of their groins, that it wants to lick and suck and eat every sweet morsel. Again and again, it will have them. A lover never satisfied, an executioner never done.

Reindeer with teeth that snarl at their prisoners, drool foaming and flowing from between each deadly fang, their eyes gleaming a menacing red that matches the bloodstains on their coarse and wiry fur. Reindeer that beat the ground with their hooves and kick at the bodies in front of them, that step on heads and hands alike, not stopping when the bodies break or pop beneath their powerful weight.

There is an awkwardness in the air as my grandpa shuffles into his office, and tells the empty, silent room, "I thought I heard you in here."

My mom and dad ask grandpa if he needs anything, maybe a nice cup of chamomile tea to calm his aging nerves, and mom leads him out of the office, my bedroom for the week, and into the kitchen.

Only I realize that it's not my grandmother that grandpa hears. It is the dry, dusty voice of Nana. I can see the shadows of her hands underneath the cot, her bright orange eyes reflecting in the twinkling white Christmas lights hanging around the door frame. Her long, crooked fingernail, black with age or earth, possibly both, or probably something beyond either, beckons for me to come, to join her.

Maybe this is the year I do. Maybe it's finally time for me to follow Nana to the enchanted North Pole. To take my promised place as Queen.

The Creaking in My Grandfather's House

I never knew my grandfather. He and my mom had a falling out before I was born and she went no contact. My grandmother had died years beforehand and my mother had no siblings, so that was it. We had no family.

I guess my father is probably still out there somewhere, but I don't even know his name. Mom refuses to talk about him.

So it was just us.

My life had been a lonely one, but 2020 was especially hard. My mom was a waitress and we were just scraping by. Then the pandemic hit and my mom was out of a job. She tried to protect me from her struggles, but I could hear her on the phone to the landlord begging for a rent extension. He couldn't legally evict us during a pandemic, but I could still hear the stress in her voice every day.

Soon we were eating cereal for breakfast, lunch, and dinner. It was kind of nice, in a way. My school had gone completely remote and my neighbor let me use his internet during the day. One of the other parents at school even lent us an old laptop, so I could still do my work. I no longer had to deal with the stress of being the poor kid in school. Of being told I was gross and that I smelled bad.

That summer had been better. Mom was able to pick up a few shifts at work, but it was hot and the protests were loud and the death and frustration of the city was boiling around us.

Fall descended slowly and the stiff humid air chilled. School continued to be virtual and I sighed with relief that I didn't have to go, but mom was laid off again and we continued to struggle.

And then, early one December morning when it was still mostly night, I heard my mom's old cell phone ring. She couldn't afford a smartphone, so she had one of those flip phones that were big before I was even in elementary school.

My grandfather was very ill and needed someone to take care of him. Mom told me she was going to go away overnight but that she'd be back in the morning.

The next morning she called to tell me that he had died. She told me she needed a week to get the arrangements in order, but to pack all my things. We were going to move into his house.

I wasn't thrilled about the idea of living in a dead man's house, but her voice was so different. The strain that had been in her words since I was an infant was gone. I wouldn't describe her as happy, I'm not sure I'd ever seen my mom happy, but she sounded…relieved.

I asked if she wanted me to attend the funeral but she refused.

"Don't worry, there won't be a service. The funeral home is going to cremate him, and I'm the only one here to mourn, so… might as well do it at home watching TV and eating ice cream with my best kid when she gets here."

The following week, mom picked me up along with our scarce possessions and took an Uber to the next town over. I had no idea my grandfather lived so close to us. All this time, all these years, he was right here.

The car pulled up to a tall thin house, the baby blue paint chipped and peeling. It was not an attractive home, but it was a lot roomier than our one-bedroom apartment.

As if she could read my thoughts, my mom leaned towards me and whispered, "You'll actually get your own bedroom."

I smiled, even though I liked my old mattress in the corner of the main area of the apartment. I was always aware of everything going on. Nothing could happen, no one could come or go without me knowing. It made me feel safe. Like I was in control.

As I walked up the walkway towards the front door, I realized just how old the house was. Wood beams flared slightly at the edges like bones and the siding was loose and falling in places.

Mom pulled out a big iron key that looked as if it were antique and unlocked the door. It swung in with a heavy groan and the hot smell of dust and mildew filled my nostrils. I flinched before following my mom inside.

"Here, come see your bedroom!" she said, excitedly.

I followed her up the creaking staircase. The house was impossibly dark for midday. It was as if we had stepped into another world. We had been out in the crisp winter air, the sun reflecting off the snow like white gold, and my eyes now refused to adjust to the dense darkness of the house.

Our apartment had been small and cheap, but the walls were white and the windows wide. It had been light and airy. This house felt old and heavy as if it were about to cave in on me. Suffocate me. Swallow me.

My mom led me to a once-white door and swung it open, the hinges whining with the force. I stepped inside to a surprisingly pleasant room. It was painted a light blue and there was a four-poster bed against one wall along with another cracked and warped door. An empty white bookcase was against the opposite side beside a small desk and chair. Across from me were two windows, recently washed so that cool light filtered through onto the floor.

I turned to face my mom, who beamed at me. "What do you think?" she asked.

"I love it. Thanks, mom."

I turned back to the room and walked towards the other door next to the bed. I opened it to reveal a thin empty closet. Wire hangers swung gently on the wooden rod, disturbed by my presence. It was the first time I ever had a closet of my own. Despite the uncomfortableness of the house, I felt a little jolt of excitement.

I was about to close the door when I noticed a large crack at the back of the closet. It was thick, almost the width of my pinkie. I couldn't see anything behind the wall but blackness. I reached out, but my hand hesitated. There was a cool breeze coming from the darkness beyond.

"Feel free to do your schooling here, or in the living room. Wherever you want, really! We were left some money, so we have our own internet and everything."

I looked back. My mom still stood in the doorway to the room, watching me. Her smile stretched to her eyes and it was so genuine, so real, it made my heartache.

My arm dropped to my side and I closed the closet door.

"Thanks, mom," I smiled back, "it's perfect."

That night, I lay in my bed wide awake, staring at the ceiling. My eyes traced the tiny cracks and fractures that lined the water stains above me as the silence of the suburbs covered me, threatening me. The familiar lulls of cars honking, people laughing, drunks shouting, were gone, replaced with an eerie silence. I looked at the windows and saw snow lazily falling past, silent as a ghost. I sighed, giving up, and put my headphones on, letting the calming noise of my music lull me to sleep.

The old house was full of the things that old people keep: half working appliances, decaying newspapers, fabrics, cans of food. Mom would go into the attic and bring down treasures to sell online, but sometimes she'd bring down something for us to keep.

Like her mother's jewelry box. The silver box was tarnished and the dark pink velvet inside was worn and stiff, but there was a lovely pair of pearl earrings and a matching necklace that she gave to me. They were beautiful, the pearls surprisingly heavy for their size. I took to wearing them every day.

"Can I look around the attic?" I asked. I wanted to explore. To pillage. To discover.

"Not yet, it's not safe. The attic was never finished properly so there's a lot of areas without a floor. I don't want you to fall through or accidentally touch the fiberglass insulation, that stuff is awful. We'll redo it once I have a decent job, but for now I'll keep bringing down the good stuff," she winked.

Life was pretty good for a time. I joined my classes online, the desk and chair much more comfortable than our old futon. My internet connection was better too, so I no longer had to worry about being disconnected or suffering through lag. My homework got easier, my grades got better. Mom looked healthy, no longer constantly worrying. She was even taking some online classes.

"I'm getting a business degree," she said while making mac and cheese, "we'll never have to suffer again." Her smile, her hope, was contagious. "You're going to graduate and go to college and it'll all work out."

Mid-January marked our sixth week in the house. The walls were cold to the touch and frost crept through the cracks in the windows. The old metal radiators hissed and complained throughout the days and nights, but they provided little warmth. I lay in my bed, heavy with moth-eaten quilts mom had found in the attic, yet the cold bit at my exposed nose and lips.

It was too cold to reach a hand out for my headphones and so I lay there in the deathly silence of the snowy winter suburbs. I inhaled deeply, the air stinging the delicate skin inside of my nostrils. I was going to learn to accept the silence. To embrace my new life. The old house sighed and whined around me, its bones cracking as it stretched as if it were readying itself for sleep as well.

The ceiling groaned above me, shifting. I buried myself deeper under the covers and tried to calm myself. Tried to remind myself that this was our home. Our fresh start. That mom was happy. That we were doing well.

I closed my eyes tight and tried to ignore the steady creaking that surrounded me as I waited for sleep.

"That's just how old homes are, love," my mom smiled as she flipped a pancake, "they breathe and settle, just like us."

That afternoon, I sat at my laptop reading, my math homework forgotten beside me. I was so engrossed that I didn't notice the album I had been listening to was over. The room was quiet, the radiator taking a silent pause between coughing fits.

Above me, a groan echoed through the floorboards. My attention snapped away from the computer and I looked up. I could see the wood in the ceiling fall and rise with another groan as if someone was walking across the attic.

I walked to the window and looked down at the driveway. The old Subaru my mother had bought weeks prior was nowhere to be seen. She was still out running errands.

The footsteps continued above my head and I turned towards my open bedroom door. I would've heard someone walk past me, I would've seen them. Swallowing my fear, I walked cautiously over, trying to step as lightly as possible. I peered out and looked up at the outline of the attic door above my head. The dirty white cord hung loosely down, swaying slightly in the drafty hallway.

The footsteps had stopped. It was as if they were waiting. As if we all were: me, the house, and the boogeyman in the attic.

Suddenly the radiator behind me hissed to life. I gasped with surprise and turned back to the empty room.

I inhaled deeply, setting my resolve, and stepped forward towards the attic. I pulled on the cord, opening the door with a loud squeak. I stopped and waited, listening intently for anything, for anyone, to react. When nothing happened, I swallowed and continued to pull the door open. The ladder fell to the carpet with a dull thud and, ignoring my mom's warnings, I began to climb up slowly.

I thought I could hear a slight rasping - wind catching a small hole or crack in the windows far off in the distance. As I climbed, I squinted into the darkness, trying to force my eyes to adjust.

A white face emerged into view, its black mouth opened in a silent scream. Red bloodshot eyes, unnaturally large, brimmed with sticky tears. It reached a white skeletal hand towards me and I screamed, falling backward onto the floor, my breath catching with the force.

Without thinking, I turned and ran. I ran past my bedroom and to the main stairs, taking two at a time. I jumped the last four steps and landed on the entranceway floor with a painful jolt through my right ankle just as my mom opened the front door. I jumped towards her, grabbing her in a violent hug as I knocked the bags from her hands. It was then that I realized I was sobbing.

"There's someone--someTHING in the attic!" I cried.

"What?" my mother asked, confused.

I swallowed the air desperately as I tried to explain, "I heard… I heard noises..." I panted, "I...I opened the door and someone was there! Someones in the attic!"

Her arms wrapped around me and hugged me tight as she began to coo at me, brushing the wet hair from my sweaty forehead.

"It's ok, sweetie! I'm sure it was just the light playing tricks on you," she kissed my temple, "tell you what, I'll go up and double-check that everything's alright, ok?"

My breathing steadied as she calmed me and after several minutes, I released her, nodding.

"I'll be right back."

I continued to try and steady my breathing as I listened to her climb the ladder. After a few minutes, she called back down, "I don't see anyone, love! I think you just scared yourself."

After a thorough investigation, she made me a cup of tea and lectured me about how I was still getting used to the new house.

I nodded dumbly, but I knew what I saw.

The imprint of the white face haunted me through the halls of the ancient home. I'd smell foul breath as the windows whispered to me and the heaters hissed. I'd hear tapping on the ceiling above me in the bathroom, or hear whispering as I lay in bed, trying to sleep.

I grew to hate the house and its noises. Its complaints and moans were like quiet threats. The sounds of humans seemed to dissipate, my mother and I silent ghosts that haunted the corners and in-between places of the house. Even my music could not penetrate it.

We sat eating dinner in silence. The dining room table was made of dark wood that shone in the dull yellow light above us and the chair beneath my back was stiff and uncomfortable. Mom had gotten rid of a lot of my grandparent's things, but this room was mostly untouched. The china cabinet behind my mother stood tall and proud, showcasing fragile plates with delicate pink roses around the edges. "Ring around the Rosie" started playing in my head.

Beside me was a low thin table with an old grey doily on top. In the fading light, I could see faint rectangles in the dull floral wallpaper where pictures or paintings used to hang.

"What was it like living here?" I asked, my words breaking the silence like glass.

Mom shrugged and ate a bite of her mashed potatoes, "Eh, not very interesting."

"Where did you put all the pictures?" I gestured to the naked walls.

"In the attic. They're just a bunch of old photos of people long gone."

"Can I see a photo of your parents?"

Mom hesitated, looking down at her half-empty plate, "Sure, I'll look for one in the attic tomorrow."

I nodded and continued to eat, our meal sinking back into quiet.

That night, I pulled the covers up to my eyes as the house shifted and groaned. It swayed around me, threatening to topple down. Dark shadows stretched from my windows. Small spots began to swell and shrink above me on the ceiling and as I focused, I realized it was the footsteps. They had returned.

I watched the feet pass above my head and stop. I tried to push myself as deep into the mattress as I could, my eyes glued to the spot where the ceiling slightly dipped. This was not my imagination.

The bulge in the ceiling grew, spreading like spilt water. I stared at it, willing it to move, to leave, to do anything.

The radiator's hiss died suddenly and the room was silent. Almost silent, except for the howls in the trees. No, it wasn't a howl. It was quiet, but not because it was outside and distant. It was a moan. A human moan.

I strained my ears and I could make out a word.

"Amber."

I screamed and lept from the bed, running blindly through the dark to my mother's room. She blinked confused as I threw on her light and began to ramble to her about what I had seen and heard, my words falling on top of each other like grain in a silo.

"A voice! A voice! I heard a voice! In the attic! It said your name!"

"Shhh, shhh," mom held her arms open for me and brought me to her chest, cradling me as if I were a small child. I cried on her shoulder and for the first time since I was a toddler, I spent the night in her bed.

In the cold light of morning, the house was still and quiet again, but I loathed it.

"We should sell it," I said at breakfast, my scrambled eggs
untouched.

"Sell what?" mom asked, scrolling through her new smartphone.

"The house. We should sell it and buy something smaller.
Something newer."

She looked up at me, her eyebrows drawn together with worry.
"Is this because of those nightmares you've been having?"

"They're not nightmares! There's something in this house.
Something in the attic."

Mom put down her phone and rested her hand on mine, "Love,
there's nothing in the attic, ok? It's just an ol--"

"Old house, I know, I know. I've heard it before." I yanked
my hand from hers and pushed my chair out roughly. "I wish I
had friends so I could go stay with them. Or a dad or someone,
anyone! I hate it here." I stormed to my room and slammed
the door.

I stood there leaning against the now-familiar wood, breathing
hard. I was trapped. This house was four times bigger than
our old apartment and yet I was stuck in a way I had never
been before. I felt claustrophobic. I needed to get out of here,
even if just for an hour.

A walk, I thought, as I opened my closet door. I reached towards a sweater when my hand froze. There was a faint tapping coming from the back wall of the closet. I looked out to
the windows beside me, to the tall dark trees that littered our
front yard. None were close enough to the wall for it to be a
branch. And, I realized with dread, the closet was at the center
of the house. That wall wasn't exposed to the outside at all.

The tapping continued. I swallowed, my fear more manageable
in the light of day. Pushing my clothes aside, I revealed the
crack that stretched behind them on the wall.

There was a shadow now. Faint and still, but I could see it. I brought my eye to the crack, my sight focusing and unfocusing on something right in front of me. And then I heard it, the rattling of a breath.

"Amber," it breathed, and suddenly my eye focused on black cracked lips and grey teeth. "Amber."

I jumped back, panic rising, but I swallowed my scream and turned to the door. I was not imagining it.

Pretending to be less afraid than I was, I turned and walked with determination to the hallway. I opened the attic door, the joints groaning till they extended fully with a loud crash.

"Marcy?" my mom called from where she still sat in the kitchen.

Ignoring her, I pulled down the ladder and climbed up.

The acrid scent of mold and urine hit me. The attic was cold, very cold, and the smell clawed at my sinuses.

The room, as long as the full house, was dimly lit by two circular windows on either end. In front of me were worn, collapsing boxes and cobwebbed chests. A wardrobe stood half-open beside a twin bed, complete with a stained mattress. A path between the junk lay before me and I followed it.

I passed piles of dusty books and a rusted bike, an antique writer's desk and lumpy trash bags. As I passed a thick pile of old frames stacked against a wall, I stopped dead. I bent down and looked at the photograph that had caught my eye. A man and woman stood in front of the very house I was in, a small girl in front of them. They had their hands on her shoulders. I recognized the face of the man, even if it was decrepit now.

"Grandpa?" I said, but the attic remained silent.

I could hear my mother's voice getting louder behind me, down in the house. I continued forward. I walked to the far wall, right where my bedroom was on the floor below me and saw what my mother had meant before - in the last two feet where the floor should meet the roof was nothing. Just blackness. And there, in the darkness, a white face looked up at me.

"Amber," it said, its voice quiet.

"Nice try, dad." I jumped, not having realized mom had already caught up to me. She rested her hand on my arm and guided me out of her way. She bent forward, "Here, sweetie, can you give me a hand?"

I blinked as I tried to figure out what she was asking. She sighed, "Nevermind, I've got it. He's pretty light these days." She reached for him and put her arms under his armpits, groaning with effort as she slowly lifted his frail body onto the floor.

His eyes never left mine. "Amber."

"That's not Amber." Mom said as she half lead, half carried him back to the twin bed I had passed. I followed her dumbly and watched as she picked up ropes from each leg of the bed I hadn't noticed before and began to tie his arms down.

The old man continued to stare at me, large tears tracing the wrinkles in his cheeks.

"He's not dead," I said. My voice surprisingly calm, flat. I felt numb.

Mom finished tying the ropes and stood. "Not yet. But soon."

"You tied him up in the attic."

"Yeah, trust me. It's more than he deserves. He should be rotting in hell." I had never heard my mom speak with such venom as she did now. I looked from the pathetic shell of my grandfather to her. Her eyes were narrowed and her mouth curved into a vicious sneer. She hated this man with all her being.

"But I figured I'd let him live for a little bit. Keep cashing his pension checks. I had hoped you wouldn't find out." She turned and reached out a hand to me. I let her fingers brush my cheek. She smiled and cradled my face, "I just wanted you to enjoy your childhood for a little bit."

She waited for a moment as if I would smile and tell her everything is alright, but I just stared. The numbness was waning and I was beginning to feel ill.

She frowned and dropped her arm. "Look, I know you probably disagree with what I did. I mean, who wouldn't. But you don't know him like I do. You don't know…" she looked away, her voice lowering to almost a whisper, "what he did."

"What did he do?"

She shook her head and began to walk towards the ladder. "Do with this what you want. Call the police on me. Save him. Whatever. It's up to you."

And she was gone, disappearing through the trap door. I turned to the old man, my grandfather. His eyes pleaded to me, those big wet sticky tears still falling down his face. I walked to him and looked down. He was so small, so weak.

His eyes flickered down to my neck and my hand automatically went up, the pearls of my necklace cool and comforting to the touch.

Red flowed into his pale cheeks and his forehead creased with sudden anger. "Are those Meredith's pearls!?" his voice rose, louder than seemed possible only seconds before. "Are those her pearls!? You slut! How dare you wear your saint of a mother's pearls! You disgusting dirty bitch!" He lunged for me, but the rope my mom tied around his wrists held. I stepped back, hitting my shoulder on the wardrobe behind me.

Hot tears burned my face as I turned and left.

The attic door closed with a bang, cutting off the old man's screams. I swallowed the bile that rose at the back of my throat and followed the muffled sobs coming from my mom's bedroom.

She was lying on the queen bed in the fetal position, crying into a pillow. I walked up and laid down behind her, gripping her arm in mine. I pulled her to me and held her tightly. Her sobs quieted but did not stop.

We stayed like that till her sobs faded to sniffles, which soon morphed into gentle snores. I stayed awake, listening to her steady breath, ignoring the creaks of my grandfather's house around me.

I Should've Known

I should've known something was off about Juniper.

For starters, her name was Juniper. That should have been my first red flag. But when her photo popped up on Tinder, my thumb hesitated over her face. Yeah, it was a bathroom selfie and yeah, her lips were pursed in an annoying semi-duck face, but fuck she was hot.

My thumb slid across my phone's screen as I swiped right.

Our first date was at a bar near her work, somewhere in Midtown. She wanted to meet up on a Tuesday. I'd have preferred a weekend night, but whatever. I'm flexible.

When the catch is hot enough...

It was some douchey place with a sports reference for a name. Foreplay or something. The place was filled with frat-boy-now-financial-advisors taking advantage of the happy hour specials and attractive bartenders in tight tank tops.

I grabbed us a table in the back, behind the giant Jenga and pool tables.

My phone buzzed with a text message: Running late. Be there in 10.

I rolled my eyes and took a sip of my cheap lager. She better be worth it.

My beer caught in my throat as she walked past the bar into the main seating area. She scanned the room for me, her long blonde hair over one shoulder. She wore a fitted button-up shirt, unbuttoned at the top, and a pencil skirt. Her long thin legs ended in a pair of pink pumps. A little bit of spice in an otherwise fairly conservative business outfit. I felt my groin warm as my eyes lingered on her calves.

Her face lit up with recognition when she caught my gaze. Her Tinder picture didn't do her justice. Her nose and chin were round, her face an oval with a slight widow's peak. Her lips were full and rosy pink. Her blue eyes wide with excitement. I raised my glass and smiled my most charming first date smile.

Five hours later, I lay in her bed empty and satisfied. Overall, a decent first date. As I listened to the water running from Juniper's bathroom, I decided with drowsy comfort that she would make a great sacrifice.

We dated for a few months. Juniper was hot, cheeky, and wild in the bedroom. Things were going great. Until she invited me to her parent's cabin for Christmas.

My father passed away earlier that year, so no one was waiting for me. I had to keep Juniper close for this year's offering and I figured it was the season of family. As they say, the more the merrier.

We weren't able to drive up to her family cabin till Christmas eve. Juniper worked as a legal secretary and the office didn't give her much time off, so it wasn't till around 3 pm before we were loading Juniper's luxury crossover. It's ok, I thought. Still plenty of time.

She wove the car through snowy back roads and explained to me what a "snow tire" was. I had only recently moved up north from Florida and I thanked Christ she didn't ask me to help drive. But I had never seen snow before and its beauty struck me. I watched out the window as we passed the sparkling white landscape, mesmerized.

Her parents, both lawyers, were loaded so I don't know why I was surprised when we pulled up to the "family cabin." The two-story mini-mansion was built from polished wood and stone. Large columns stretched up from the ground to the roof, creating a sharp awning that sheltered the double glass front doors and floor-to-ceiling windows that spotted the modern exterior.

Juniper parked her car at the top of the driveway, expressing obvious annoyance that all three spaces in the garage were already taken by her parents' and sisters' cars.

I peered out the passenger window at the house. Large soft snowflakes fell lazily to the ground, illuminated by two spotlights shining from the front yard onto the cabin's facade. The light reflected off the snow, giving it the illusion that the heavens were raining gold.

"Wow, I know I'm from Florida, but…" I paused, "this isn't really what I was picturing."

Juniper lowered onto the wheel to get a better look at her family home. Her face glowed in the warm light from outside. She chuckled, "Yeah, I know. But don't be fooled, it's not all fancy." She eyed me mischievously, "The cell service is fucking shit."

"Ah." I nodded as if that one fact brought her whole family back down to earth.

"You brought your swimsuit, right?"

I laughed at the joke. "Oh, of course."

Her smile fell. "No, Calvin, I'm serious. You brought your suit, right?"

I looked out at the snowy wilderness around us, unsure how to respond.

Juniper sighed, "For the jacuzzi! I'm sure my dad has an extra pair you can borrow. It might be big on you, but it'll do."

"Oh, great," I said without much enthusiasm.

Big wet snowflakes coated us in the few minutes it took to unload the car and jog to the house. The door closed with a thud and Juniper dropped her bags, kicking off her pristine duck boots before bounding down the hallway.

"Amber, Clover, where are you guys?!"

I placed the box of meticulously wrapped gifts I had been carrying down and grabbed a quick look at my watch. 5:14. Perfect. The ride up was faster than I had expected. Still plenty of time.

I looked around to see that I was standing in an entrance room. The wood floor and walls glowed with the yellow light radiating from a huge chandelier hanging above my head. It was made of light grey branches braided around each other, their bark smooth and manicured as if they had naturally grown that way.

Feminine squeals rang down the hall from the back of the house. I stood there, awkwardly unsure what to do. At least I looked the part. Juniper, dissatisfied with my wardrobe, had bought me a tan wool coat. She explained that my faded leather jacket was neither weather-appropriate nor fashionable. I had moved up to the city during the summer and my closet hadn't been prepared for the blistering winds and snow of the north. I'm lucky I had Juniper to help with that. At least according to her.

Snow clung to the shoulders of the department store coat as the warmth of the house embraced me. I could feel the chilly wetness of melting snow sink into my knit beanie. A matching scarf was wrapped around my neck, the fibers clinging to my moist lips unpleasantly.

I grabbed at the scarf with my gloved hand and pulled. In my defense, I wasn't used to the lack of individual fingers and the clumsiness of a hand wrapped in thick wool. I had half of the unwieldy piece of clothing in one hand while the end hugged my throat tightly when the Mills family entered.

"Oh no! Baby!" Juniper's voice was filled with amusement as she rushed to help me. She took the scarf and carefully untangled it from my neck.

A gravelly voice boomed, filling the space, "June mentioned you were from the south! Guess you guys don't really need winter accessories down there, huh?"

Juniper continued to help me undress out of my winter outwear as I turned. Behind her stood a beast of a man. He towered over my 5'11" frame, his shoulders broader than a football player's. His beard was thick yet neatly trimmed. He wore a fitted flannel shirt and pressed jeans, making him look more like a lumberjack who modeled for L.L. Bean on his off days than a lawyer.

My mouth hung open for a moment before I regained my composure. "Mr. Mills, it's nice to meet you." I extended my hand around Juniper, who was still working on my coat. "I'm Calvin."

"Matthias, Matthias!" He roared joyously, pushing Juniper out of the way as he pulled me into a tight embrace. My body was engulfed by his meaty chest. I'm not ashamed to admit it, it was the best hug of my life. Comforting and warm. For a moment, I forgot about the greater good. My purpose in life. My father. It was like being suspended in a vat of Christmas and love.

He let go of me and I stepped back, noticing for the first time the two figures behind him.

"Calvin, these are my sisters: Clover and Amber," Juniper said, beaming from me to them.

Juniper was the middle daughter of three. Clover, at twenty-nine, was the eldest and Amber, at twenty-two, was the youngest. The only thing the sisters had in common was that they were three of the most gorgeous women I had ever seen in my life. Clover had silky black hair, cut short at her chin. Her features were sharp, her thin grey eyes bordered by heavy eyelashes. She smiled coyly at me as she extended her hand.

"Nice to meet you, Calvin." While Juniper's voice was high and bubbly, Clover's was low and throaty. Similar to her father's but with a husky feminine quality that made it difficult to think of her as my girlfriend's sister.

"And I'm Amber." A soft voice said to my left. I tore my gaze away from Clover to the younger sister. Amber was much shorter than her siblings with thick red hair and a circular face. She had a button nose and round green eyes. She looked like she had stepped out of an Irish folktale. Amber contrasted sharply with her sisters. Juniper was tall and had an athletic build. Tight but soft, firm and preppy like a cheerleader. Clover was tall and thin, angles and bite, the only one in the room who actually looked like a lawyer (but ironically was a painter).

And Amber.... well... let's just say Amber's curves swelled and ebbed in all the right places. A sailor could get lost exploring those rolling waves.

I smiled and took her hand. "It's a pleasure to meet you." Juniper didn't talk about her family much and I knew well enough not to ask, but I made a mental note to discreetly broach the subject of whether she and her sisters all had the same parents. "Where's Mrs. Mills?"

Matthias' smile wavered. "Eh, she had to run an errand." His eyes shifted to Clover, whose returning gaze narrowed slightly. His dark eyes shot back to mine and he smiled confidently again, the moment of weirdness over as suddenly as it had started. "She'll be back later."

"Come on, Juniper. Help us with dinner!" Amber said as she grabbed her sister's hand and began to pull her down the hall.

Clover's mouth turned downwards as her dark eyes lingered on me for a moment before following her sisters.

Something heavy hit my shoulder and I jumped. Matthias had clapped his huge hand onto my back. "Let me tell you, it's nice to have a man to talk with! I'm always surrounded by women!" He laughed a low good-hearted growl as he led me into another room.

We entered a cavernous living room, the ceiling arching high above us. Several thick naked wooden beams held it up. A large red oriental rug stretched from wall to wall, complimenting the forest green walls well. Two large brown leather couches sat kitty-corner to each other in the middle of the room.

The walls were lined with hunting trophies. The taxidermied heads of different animals stared out across at each other, their dead glassy eyes unseeing. Deer and bears snarled meaning-lessly, their teeth barred without emotion. A bobcat perched on a rock in the corner of the room next to a fat pheasant. Against one wall was a large glass gun rack. Polished rifles gleamed in the warm overhead light. The centerpiece of the room, a massive moose head, rested above the marble fireplace in which a large fire roared, radiating heat and golden light around the room.

Catching me eyeing his collection, Matthias laughed, "are you a hunter, Calvin?"

I thought for a second before carefully choosing my next words. "My father and I used to go hunting once a year together. I still practice the tradition."

"Good." His deep voice resonated with the warmth from the fireplace, creating an atmosphere of masculine comfort and safety. "I like a man who hunts."

I smiled at him and nodded, unsure how to respond.

"Sit down, sit down!" he ordered as he fell into one of the couches. I obliged, sitting on the other couch facing him as I prepared for the inevitable father-boyfriend interview.

"Calvin…" he rolled my name around his tongue experimentally as he eyed me. "That's a Protestant name, isn't it?"

"Uh…" I stammered, taken off guard. "Yeah, I guess so."

Matthias leaned forward, resting his forearm against his thigh. "Do you believe in God, Calvin?"

The line of questioning was going down a dark path I had not expected. In the four months I had been dating Juniper, she had never brought up religion.

"Of course…" My answer was slow and deliberate.

Matthias nodded, his eyes narrowing at me. "God is the most important thing to this family. The Mills clan walks close with Him. We are His servants, and we take that role very seriously."

I nodded. "My family believed the same. We were very devout."

"Were?" Matthias asked.

"My father died this past February. I never knew my mother, but my dad raised me to be fearful of God."

"And what do you believe now?"

I hesitated, "I still practice."

"You can be honest with me, Calvin." Matthias sat back into the thick leather couch. "I won't tell Juniper not to date you because of your religious beliefs. Or lack thereof." He laughed as if that last part was a joke.

I smiled at him, "I'll admit, I don't follow the more embellished of the ceremonies my father taught me but I still believe in his word and actions."

Matthias nodded. "I can respect that. I know my daughters only participate in some of the more, how did you put it… embellished of the ceremonies solely for my benefit. I understand the younger generation doesn't care as much for the ritual of worship. But I think it's important that you know how deep this family's spirituality runs. God comes first in this house. When God asks us to do something," he paused, looking towards the floor as he cleared his throat. He looked back up at me, his gaze fierce, freezing me in time and space. "We obey without question."

"As it should be," I said.

We stared at each other for several moments before the tension was broken by Matthias' deep laughter.

"I like you, Calvin." He stood. "I'm gonna go grab a beer, want one?"

"That'd be great, thanks."

He left and I sat in the living room, surrounded by fire and death.

Dinner and drinks passed uneventfully. The food was delicious and Matthias' wine cellar was impressive. I didn't even notice the absence of Mrs. Mills throughout the course of the meal. Matthias kept filling my glass and I drank the rich red wine with relish.

I should've known better. Christmas eve had been me and my father's night, so maybe my overindulgence was an attempt to deal with his absence. Maybe I wasn't ready to go through that night's rite without him just yet. But I knew at the back of my mind that I had to. That it was my duty. I owed it not just to my father, but to the world.

As Matthias poured another glass of wine, I looked down at my watch. 9:58. I needed to pace myself. To rest. I'd need my wits and strength for the witching hour. Luckily, I did not have to excuse myself early. As the clock struck ten, Matthias raised his glass in cheer.

"Let us bless our last sip of wine before we head to bed," his eyes twinkled with drink, "tonight's a big night for us, so let us toast to family" he held his glass towards me, "and new friends. To endings and new beginnings." he winked, his smirk lopsided. "To the most sacred holiday, and to God. Let us give to Him all that He asks of us, and hope He favors us with the treasures of His bounty."

He stretched his glass to mine. "To Saint Nicholas." Our wine glasses clinked as the sisters' voices echoed their father. "To Saint Nicholas!"

I laughed and drowned the last of my wine, attributing each and every red flag to the quirkiness of a rich and spoiled family of lawyer lumberjacks.

I awoke later that night to hands running up my chest. I opened my eyes, my mind groggily trying to catch up to my body's instant reaction. A warm naked body pressed into me and I rolled towards her, pulling her closer. My lips found her soft skin and I kissed her neck, tracing the gentle curve to her jaw. Something brushed lightly against the back of my neck, but my brain was too drenched in desire and sleep to register the sensation. She moaned and I ran my hand up her side. As I cupped her breast, the supple flesh gave under my fingertips and electricity shot through my body as I squeezed. Bringing my mouth to hers, I kissed her deeply

Arms wrapped around my back and I opened my eyes with instant focus, my vision suddenly filled with Clover's cold grey gaze.

I recognized the sensation of breasts much larger than Juniper's or Clover's pressing against my back, firm and soft. Amber's breath was hot on my ear. "Shhhh, don't fight it." Her tongue slid across the sensitive skin at the top of my neck and brought my earlobe between her lips. She sucked softly and my dick swelled.

I turned to face her, her lips finding mine as I pressed myself into her thighs. I moaned lightly as Clover's hand snaked around my hip. As I kissed Amber, Clover moved to my cock, gently teasing it before wrapping her fingers around the shaft.

"Oh, fuck." I gasped as she began to stroke. I rolled onto my back, my eyes closed as Amber and Clover explored my body, their heat radiating into my sides.

Clover kissed my cheek and whispered, "Open your eyes."

I obeyed.

Above me, standing at the foot of the bed, was a woman. I sat bolt upright, filled with sudden panic. Clover and Amber's hands fell away as they watched my reaction with amused expressions on their faces.

The woman stood, looking at me. Her hair was long, longer than Juniper's, and it was stark white. Not graying but pure white. She stood completely naked, her pale body glowing in the silver light of the moon outside the window. Her eyes were wide, revealing pupils completely milky with cataracts. She looked ageless, color fading from her along with her youth, yet her fair skin was still smooth and firm.

"Calvin, mom. Mom, Calvin." Clover cooed beside me, her voice a mix of sensuality and power.

Mrs. Mills stared at me with those unseeing eyes, and she smiled.

"It's nice to meet you, Calvin," she said quietly, her voice delicate.

I was breathing heavily, my panting shifting from arousal to fear in mere seconds. My fight or flight instinct was screaming at me to do something, but I was frozen. My eyes darted to the digital clock on the nightstand. 11:28. My alarm was set to go off in only a few minutes. I still had time to prepare for the ritual. I looked up at Mrs. Mills, who was still smiling at me, waiting for a response.

My voice came out strained, tight with fear, confusion, and some embarrassment at the sheer amount of nudity around me. "You too, Mrs. Mills."

"Please, call me Holly." Without waiting for a response, she turned to Clover. "He will do. Prepare him for sacrifice."

I felt a pinch in my neck, then darkness.

I opened my eyes slowly. My head throbbed and my body was shaking uncontrollably, the air shockingly cold. I tried to take in the scene around me through blurry vision. I was sitting on the cold hard ground. Short walls of snow surrounded me in a circle, but the circle itself was bare except for dozens of thick white candles. My ass cheeks were numb against the frozen leaves that had only recently been covered. I was naked and I realized the Mills family was kneeling around me.

Juniper and her sisters swayed in the chill night air, the slowly falling snow soaking into the delicate fabric of their night-gowns. They chanted together, their voices joining in a chorus of a German-sounding dialect I did not recognize.

Directly in front of me stood Matthias. His hands clasped in front of him as if in prayer. A black, crooked dagger jutted out from his grasp towards his face.

Jesus fuck, what time is it? I thought as I tried to stand, but my hands were tied behind my back.

A creature stepped out from the chilly darkness and into the circle. It loomed above me, casting a shadow over my freezing body.

It was a reindeer, Holly straddling its back. She wore a long, flowing white gown. A crown of icicles was perched on her forehead and she looked down, her white eyes glowing in the candlelight.

Contrasting starkly to Holly's disturbing beauty, the reindeer was twisted and distorted. It looked more like someone's idea of a sick joke than a living animal. Instead of standing on hooves, the deer's leg bones protruded from the ends of red oozing stumps. Bloody velvet hung loosely from white bones in fleshy strips. Its face was dirty and blackened with what looked like charcoal. A long, black tongue lolled out of its mouth between two rows of human teeth.

I squirmed in the rope that bound me, trying to pull the knots loose. Juniper and I had played with bondage in the bedroom and I knew her style. It wouldn't take me long to undo anything she had done and my adrenaline silenced any doubt that it could have been any one of the other four family members.

The creature stepped forward towards me as it spoke, its exposed ankle bone pressing into the frozen earth with a dull crunch.

"I am the soul of Saint Nicholas," it roared, its voice cracking through the air like thunder.

I paused my squirming. "I'm sorry, what?"

"You heard him, mortal!" Holly shrieked. Her voice had lost the fragile air from before. It was now dry and harsh, like paper crinkling into a ball. Or wood cracking as fire bites into it. It didn't sound real. More like a demon's voice than a human's. Like a succubus or siren. High pitched and flittering. The cackle of an evil witch.

My fight against the rope renewed with desperate determination. Fuck this shit and fuck this family.

The reindeer snickered quietly before beginning to speak again. "I am weak and old, but fresh blood will wash me anew." His eyes glowed like burning coals.

"Oh Saint Nicholas, we worship thee!" The voices of the Mills family rose above the circle, their eyes closed with intense concentration.

Matthias continued, "We call upon the witching hour to bring our deity new life!"

"Let Saint Nicholas live again!" The daughters chanted.

The rope fell loosely from my wrists and I silently thanked my now ex-girlfriend's crappy survival skills. I jumped up, naked and filled with a fury that easily squashed all self-doubt I had going into this cursed holiday. My father's death was far from my mind, replaced with hatred.

Matthias' eyes shot open. His daughters' chanting faded as they looked from him to me to the god before us.

I looked at my watch. 11:58. I sighed with relief. Witching Hour wasn't for another three hours. I had plenty of time to deal with the Mills' shenanigans before it was too late to complete the ritual.

The reindeer, who now stood almost a foot beneath me, smiled. "Oh, the foolish confidence of the son charged with the burden of the father," he bellowed, his voice deep and impressive.

I looked down at him, our eyes locking. "What did you say?"

The deer began to paw the ground, shifting right and left. He looked like a child doing the pee-pee dance. "Oh, look at me," he said in a mocking tone. "I'm Calvin and I'm an orphan. My daddy entrusted me with our family's sacred duty but I'm scared." The reindeer shook its head dramatically with each word, "If only daddy was here to help me kill these people."

Holly's anger faltered on her face. She was confused as well. This behavior, apparently, was not what the Mills family expected from their god.

"What the-" Matthias stood, his face twisted in confusion.

"Get the fuck off me, lady." The reindeer bucked and Holly fell to the ground with a painful thud. Matthias reached out and quickly pulled her towards him. His daughters were now cowering at his sides. All malice and power gone from their faces, replaced with utter confusion.

How do you like it? Fucking assholes.

The reindeer continued, "Luckily for little Calvin, the Mills are too dumb to know that the witching hour isn't midnight. Little Calvin still has hours to kill all of them and burn their black little hearts in a fire born of coal and pine."

He stopped his dance, his face becoming stern again. "You must've been thrilled when you were brought to the woods. No fake Christmas for Florida boy, oh no. No mail order pine needles and coal for daddy's little boy. No, you thought coming up north was the right thing to do. Not like daddy made you live somewhere where it didn't snow for a reason."

I spat at the ground and looked at the Mills. "This isn't fucking Santa Claus, you dim fucks."

The reindeer took a step towards me. "Do you believe in fate, Calvin?"

I looked down at him. "How did you find me? How… how are you even mortal?"

He leaned forward, his dead animal lips hovering by my face. "I followed you, Calvin. I could smell your hunter scent in the snow and I followed it." He stepped back and looked up at me, smirking. "I found the same idiots I knew you would. A little early Christmas gift, just for you." His long tongue stretched out towards me. I flinched as the dry leathery skin touched my face, caressing me. It smelt of dried fish and dirt.

"How were you able to become corporeal?" I asked, shooing his tongue away from me. It fell lifeless, hanging in front of him uselessly.

He turned his head to look at the Mills family, who stood behind him, mouths agape. Juniper's mascara ran and she cried, confused at the scene in front of her. My mind shot back to Matthias' gun rack. His hunting trophies on the wall.

"Oh god, he made this vessel for you? Fucking sick, man."

The reindeer shrugged. Or at least, he lifted his shoulders in what could be interpreted as a shrug.

"So what now," I asked, "are you going to kill me?"

"Not tonight, Calvin." He winked.

I looked down at my watch. 1:15.

"I still have two hours to perform the ritual…" There was a hiss around me, like sand flowing. I looked up to see a pile of black where the Mills family had been seconds before.

The reindeer swung his face around, as if in astonishment. "Oh my! Where did those rascals get to!?!" He stomped around in mock confusion, the bare bones he stood on audibly snapping with the weight.

"Welp," he looked back up at me, "good luck trying to find new sacrifices in the middle of bum fuck whatever state this is. I'm out." He turned away from me and leapt into the snow. He bounded deeper into the woods, his legs spasming in front of him as if he didn't have the right number of knees.

"See you next Christmas Eve, mother fucker!" He said over his shoulder as he disappeared from sight.

And now, because of the idiocy of one family, my legacy has died. For the first time in 200 years, my bloodline has failed in our sacred duty.

And for that, I apologize. I have failed you. There were so many signs, so many red flags. I should've known.

So here's a warning, the last thing I can offer you in my father's name. This Christmas Eve, make sure to lock your doors and windows. Leave your shoes outside and stay bundled in your bed. Because this year, Krampus is back.

Trigger Warning Appendix

CHILD ABUSE & DEATH

The Twelve Days of Christmas

I was a Christmas Elf

Author Bio

Jess Charle lives in the NYC area and cohabits with her husband, Josiah and her bossy corgis, Ion & Digit. She is also tolerated by her two cats, Mu & Nano.

Her work has been published in the *Columbia Journal* and *Daughters of Darkness*, an all women horror anthology, as well as featured on *The NoSleep Podcas*t and *creepypasta. com*. You can find more of her writing and upcoming events on www.meltingalphabet.com.

Jess also works with film and audio, enjoys knitting, drumming, and disturbing her friends and neighbors.

Prone to nightmares and dark thoughts, she tries to make everyone's world just a little more frightening.

I wouldn't trust her if I were you...

Check out her first horror anthology, *Lost in a Nightmare*, available at Amazon, Target, and Barnes & Noble.